'What happened to us, Lorna?'

'Please don't, James,' Lorna said, because she couldn't bear it—she wanted to turn to him like a flower to the sun, wanted to curl up in his lap and let him stroke her hair as they watched the movie, or lie on the sofa wrapped in his arms and not worry about the ending. Only she couldn't. 'Please don't start about that.'

Kiss me. She wouldn't say it, wouldn't kiss him again, but every cell in her body screamed it. And their cries were heeded, because his mouth did find hers and, for Lorna, the bliss of familiar lips on hers brought a shock of comfort. Shock because every nerve jumped as their master flicked the switch and declared he was home, and comfort because his kiss had always been wondered about, always been sought but never found in others.

Carol Marinelli recently filled in a form where she was asked for her job title and was thrilled, after all these years, to be able to put down her answer as 'writer'. Then it asked what Carol did for relaxation, and after chewing her pen for a moment Carol put down the truth—'writing'. The third question asked—'What are your hobbies?' Well, not wanting to look obsessed or, worse still, boring, she crossed the fingers on her free hand and answered 'swimming and tennis'. But, given that the chlorine in the pool does terrible things to her highlights, and the closest she's got to a tennis racket in the last couple of years is watching the Australian Open, I'm sure you can guess the real answer!

Also out this month is Carol's fabulous, sensationally sexy Modern™ Romance BLACKMAILED INTO THE GREEK TYCOON'S BED

EMERGENCY: WIFE LOST AND FOUND

BY
CAROL MARINELLI

MILLS & BOON
Pure reading pleasure™

First published in Great Britain 2009
Large Print edition 2010
Harlequin Mills & Boon Limited,
Eton House, 18-24 Paradise Road,
Richmond, Surrey TW9 1SR

© Carol Marinelli 2009

ISBN: 978 0 263 21065 1

Printed and bound in Great Britain
by CPI Antony Rowe, Chippenham, Wiltshire

EMERGENCY: WIFE LOST AND FOUND

For Anne and Tony xxxx

CHAPTER ONE

THERE was an energised buzz in the emergency staffroom as James Morrell walked in with a long overdue mug of coffee in hand, and took a seat. A buzz that came from too much adrenaline and too many people talking at the same time...

A serious crash on the entrance ramp to the M1 motorway had transformed an already busy Friday afternoon into a chaotic one. A car had hit black ice and a nasty pile-up had ensued involving a coach and several cars. The slushy, snowy conditions had just added to the misery for the victims and the rescue squads. Several London hospitals had taken the strain, but the emergency department of North London Regional Hospital had sent out a mobile team to the scene and extra staff had been called in to assist. And now, as the clock hit five p.m. the department was just starting to catch up with the backlog. ANUM May Donnelly had ordered sandwiches and refreshments for her team and had insisted that the staff, some of whom who had been on duty since seven a.m. and would be there for a good few hours yet, actually stopped for half an hour and took a well-earned break before the department came off bypass and allowed ambulances to bring patients in instead of diverting to another hospital.

Having ensured her staff were sorted, May had rung her beloved husband and told him that again she would be late home, eternally grateful that he didn't add to her stress, just cheerfully told her he'd start dinner and reminded her that this time next year they'd be on their retirement cruise.

'Well done, guys.' James's deep voice hushed the room for a moment. 'I'll speak with you in groups over the next couple of days and go over it all—but suffice it to say for now that you all did an excellent job. The team that came out with me was top class. The firefighters and paramedics both commented on how well you all worked and well done to the students too.' He glanced over to where the student nurses sat and May Donnelly smiled to herself as she watched each girl flush pink as James Morrell looked in their direction.

It was an automatic reflex, May had long since decided. James Morrell must think that all women had a slight rosy glow to their cheeks, because that was how they generally appeared when he was around!

May had been in nursing close to forty years now and had seen plenty, could tell a few tales in her thick Irish brogue, and she could tell a few home truths too—but would these young women listen to her when she told them that they were wasting their time with James?

Not for a minute.

Tall and of solid build, he looked like a rugby

forward, minus the broken nose and cauli-
flower ears. With his straight brown hair and
piercing green eyes he cut more than a dash as
he strode through the department. He was certainly a commanding man, and unusually at
thirty-five he was single too. Having got
drenched out on the motorway, he was now
dressed in theatre blues that showed a lot of
bare arms and just a smattering of chest hair,
and there wasn't a woman in the room who
didn't notice.

'Are you coming to Mick's leaving do next
Saturday, James?' May watched as Kristy, one
of the students, attempted to ask casually.
Though it might be considered a touch forward
for a student, every female in the room was
seriously glad that she had asked. He was good-
looking, a doctor, definitely not gay—who
could blame a girl for trying?

'I might pop in for one drink.' James looked
over from the television he wasn't really
watching. He was just trying to switch his

brain off for a while—except he couldn't—even though the department had been stood down, even though the wreckage was starting to be cleared, it didn't feel over yet. There was a feeling of unease he couldn't explain. Sure, if he sat and thought about it, which he was doing right now, he could easily put it down to having just been in charge on the scene of an accident with more than forty victims, but he'd done that before—many times. No, there was this unsettled feeling as he sat there in the staffroom, especially when Abby just had to start!

'I could give you a lift!' She smiled over to him, but James didn't return it, just looked back to the TV.

'I can give you a lift if you like, James,' Abby said again, assuming he hadn't heard her offer.

Ooh, May was enjoying this. Though no one in the department would *ever* guess, May didn't like Abby, the new, rather snooty registrar, who clearly had her blue eyes set on the main prize.

'I'm fine.' *Still* James didn't turn around. 'I don't even know if I'll get there.'

'Well,' still Abby persisted, 'if you do want a drink, I'm happy to drive. It's not often we both get a Saturday night off at the same time.'

Yes-s-s! May loved listening to this—listening to Abby talk as if they were an old married couple, who weren't getting to spend enough time together.

'I've got plans next Saturday…' James did look over now and flashed his 'back off' smile that May just adored, and she watched the colour whoosh up Abby's face as very firmly, as was James's way, he put her back in her box. 'As I said, I might try to get there for one drink—I would like to say farewell to Mick!' he added, just so everyone in the room understood that the reason he was going was to say goodbye to the porter who had served the department for twenty years now. 'Who's holding onto his collection?'

'That would be me.' May said, 'but you've already contributed.'

'Sure?' James checked.

'Quite sure.' May nodded, still smiling to herself. When would these girls realize that James Morrell didn't mix business with pleasure? Mind you, had she been thirty years younger she'd have given it a go. Not that it would have done any good—in all the years she'd worked with him, he'd never been involved with a staff member, had never, not even once, brought a date along to a work do.

There was an aloofness to James that May had never quite worked out. Polite, kind, nice, he was also a closed book. He would chat about the news, current affairs, patients, he knew all his staff well and talked easily to them, just not about himself.

He was certainly sexy…certainly he liked sex!

As ANUM, or Associate Nurse Unit Manager, which used to be just plain Sister, May often had to call the consultants in from home, and a few ladies had picked up the phone or had been heard purring in the background as a rather breathless James had answered. Though he always came in promptly, and no one would have had a clue that he'd just been hauled in mid-session! Her friend Pauline did some housekeeping for him and though, like May, discretion was Pauline's rule, she only had to purse her lips on occasion when May fished a little to let May know that James had an active life outside these hospital walls. Once—May managed a slight flush at the memory—when they'd had to rapidly change to go out on the Flying Squad, James had had blood on his shirt already and had had to change in the foyer while they'd awaited the transport to take them to the accident.

Everyone probably thought she was having a hot flush as she sat there in the staffroom, fanning her cheeks, but May could still recall the sight of that broad back gouged with nail marks and when he had turned she had come face to face with a chest covered in love bites.

Phew!

'Okay, May?' James loved working with May and always looked out for her.

'Just a bit warm.' May smiled.

'They can never get it right.' James glanced out at the heavy grey sky and the slush of old snow piled up on the window. The sky was already dark but a streetlight showed a flurry of new snow falling. 'It's bloody freezing out there and they've got the heating turned up so that it's like a sauna in here.'

That restless feeling was back, his solid muscular thigh was bobbing up and down, and no matter how he tried to he was just not able to kick back and relax just yet.

'Can we accept…?' the intercom in the staff-room crackled into life.

'We're on bypass,' May immediately interrupted, because her staff needed this break. The accident had meant that for a few hours North London Regional Hospital was closed to new admissions, the ambulances automatically diverted to other hospitals, and though it was a tough call to make, it was one that *had* to be made if safe working levels were to be maintained. The department was struggling at the moment in any case. Two junior doctors had left in the middle of their six-month rotations and they had not filled the vacancies. Abby was good, but new, and one of the registrars had just gone on extended sick leave. Everyone was working beyond their limits and even more so today. They would come off bypass soon. May had, in consultation with James and the nursing supervisor, decided they would call it off in the next half an hour, but for now her staff needed to restock, not just on food and drink but the depleted store shelves, and also get a few more patients up to the wards.

But the voice was crackling on.

'She's just been found a little way from the accident scene, trapped in her car… Jane Doe, in her twenties, hypothermic, full cardiac arrest…'

James was already standing up, grabbing a handful of sandwiches and heading for the door, appalled at the thought of a patient left behind and what she must have been through.

'Accept,' he and May said together.

The late staff were already setting up for the expected new arrival as James and May rushed around. Rolling out the warming unit, which was like a large duvet that would be inflated with warm air and placed over her, IVs were being run through warmers and the anaesthetist had been paged and was running down from a no doubt frantic ICU. 'What else do we know?'

'Not much!' Lavinia, the crackling voice on the intercom, who was pretty in the flesh, brought them swiftly up to date. 'The car was found in a field a few hundred yards from the accident scene, the windscreen was shattered so she's been exposed for a while. She had a blanket around her, so it would seem she was conscious after the accident. She arrested as they freed her from the wreckage.'

'Do we have a name?'

'Not yet. She's been intubated and is on her way. ETA nine minutes.'

'Come on,' James said to May, 'let's go and meet the ambulance.'

They stood in the ambulance bay, James only in his theatre scrubs. It seemed rather inappropriate to moan about the weather—still, it was *freezing*.

He glanced at his watch and willed the ambulance to hurry up. 'Four hours in this.' He wasn't making small talk, his head was frantically trying to do the maths. Four hours exposed to freezing temperatures, and no doubt already injured from the accident. In hypothermia, patients often arrested when moved and, though it was never good news, the fact it had been a witnessed arrest was positive. 'This is going to be a long one.'

It would—her body temperature would need to be gradually raised and until her temperature was normal the resuscitation would continue. When the body was hypothermic the brain required little oxygen and there was a chance that despite being trapped for hours, despite being in full cardiac arrest, this patient might make a full recovery—and given her age, she would be afforded every benefit of the doubt.

'The poor pet, stuck out there in this blessed weather all these hours,' May said, shivering into her cardigan as they stood in the ambulance bay. She wished nurses still wore capes!

'I knew it wasn't over,' James said. 'There were so many cars involved, just so much chaos, we're going to have to review this.'

'We will,' May sighed. 'But it was already getting dark by four, and with the snow and everything...' Her voice trailed off. Security was having a row with a driver who had insisted on parking his car in the ambulance bay. His wife would only be two minutes, he was arguing loudly and, no, he wasn't moving his car, but James had already heard enough. May watched as he strode over, an imposing man at the best of times, but when someone compromised his patients' care, woe betide them. May cringed as James not too politely told the driver where he could put his car, but she smiled as he strode back.

'He thinks it's a bloody car park.'

'He doesn't now,' May pointed out, watching as the driver reversed angrily out of the ambulance bay, but her smile soon faded. 'That's all we need!'

A television news team, which was setting up a little way down to do a live cross on the evening news about the earlier incident, had got wind of the 'forgotten patient' story. They dashed over with their cameras and talked excitedly into their microphones as James told Security to bring out the screens to shield the incoming patient from prying eyes. The last thing he wanted was some kid eating their tea, seeing their mother being brought into hospital at death's door. He was taut with suppressed rage as he shooed the journalists back and helped Security to erect the screens quickly.

Oh, the joys of being an emergency consultant!

'Where the hell's the ambulance?' James demanded of May, and she glanced at her watch.

'It will be a couple more minutes yet. Are you okay, James?' May couldn't help but ask. He was like a coiled spring this afternoon. Okay, he was often brusque but there was just *something* about him now that May couldn't put her finger on.

He was about to give his usual dismissive 'Fine,' only this was May who was asking and he respected her more than anyone in the department, looked out for her in the same way that she looked out for him, and because of that he was honest.

'I don't know, May.' He could just hear the ambulance siren, which meant it was still a minute or two away. He turned to her wise, familiar face and even if it sounded evasive he answered with the truth. 'I really don't know.'

'Are you not feeling well?' She asked.

'It's not that…' He blew out a breath, long and white in the freezing early evening sky, and tried to find the right word to describe how he felt. Nervous? Anxious? Neither really fitted. He just felt uneasy, that was the best word he could come up with, but he was hardly going to offer that to May.

'I know that it's hell in the department at the moment, we're so many staff down, but…' she offered.

'It's not that either. I hate it that we missed someone. I knew it wasn't over…' His words were drowned out by the sirens and the noise of the camera crews. Security opened the back of the ambulance door before it had even halted, the driver jumped into the back and, seeing the greedy cameras, pulled the blanket over the patient's face, which was acceptable as she was already intubated, while the other paramedic pushed on her chest. The stretcher was unclipped and James took over the cardiac massage as May bagged the patient. They bumped the stretcher out of the ambulance, raised it and then set off to the resuscitation area in a skilled, practised motion.

But midway there, James lost his stride, the whole party halting for less than a second as James caught up, or seemed to.

She'd always had pretty feet.

Despite her plain clothes and serious, unmade-up face, Lorna had always worn pretty pink nail varnish just as this patient was, and Lorna had a mole just on the dorsum of her right foot too. James could feel the chest beneath his hand as he massaged the heart and he had, for that stupid second, wanted to stop the stretcher, wanted to rip the blanket from her face and find out that it wasn't her.

Except James knew with dread that it was.

A coil of wet dark auburn hair had escaped the blanket, and as they whooshed into Resus and prepared to lift her onto the hard resuscitation bed, the blanket covering her was whipped off. Then he finally got confirmation, but he'd already known for a good fifteen seconds that it was Lorna.

He'd always wondered if she'd changed. Up

in Glasgow for a conference a couple of years ago, he'd scanned the shops and bars for a woman with auburn hair and huge amber eyes. He'd told himself it was futile, that it had been so long ago she might have dyed her hair by now, she'd always hated that it was red after all—or maybe she'd have put on weight. Or, worse, he might bump into her pushing a stroller containing twins. He was being ridiculous, he had told himself that day, because even if she walked towards him, stood in front of him, he probably wouldn't even recognise her.

He'd known at the time he was kidding himself and he'd had that confirmed today.

Ten years on and he'd recognised her in an instant by her pretty feet alone.

CHAPTER TWO

'SHE WAS UNRESPONSIVE when they found her, but she had did have a pulse. She arrested when we moved her from the vehicle,' the paramedic informed them as they raced into Resus.

'Do we have an ID?'

As she transferred the patient over to the resuscitation bed it was May who asked the question when James didn't—he was still massaging the chest, even though Lavinia had offered to take over.

'From the driving licence in the car we have a Lorna McClelland, thirty-two years of age, from Scotland; she's a doctor apparently…'

'How was she missed?' It was the first time James had spoken since her arrival, and it was an irrelevant question really. She had been found, she was ill, for now all they could deal with was what presented, and May frowned as James persisted with the pointless. 'How could she have been missed?'

'I'm not sure,' the paramedic answered. 'We just got a callout twenty-five minutes ago. Mind you, it's been chaos out there.'

Instead of the emergency consultant it was Khan, the anaesthetist, who was running the show, flashing lights in the patient's eyes, frowning up at James as he checked the airway, calling for drugs, and at that moment May stepped in. She had no idea what was wrong with James, but she would find out later. He was standing there, massaging the chest, as grey as sheet metal and instead of assessing the patient and commencing active treatment, still there he stood. It happened now and then, May knew that well, where staff just hit a wall. But maybe it was another peril of working in Emergency that was occurring here, May thought as she watched the beads form on his brow. He knew this patient!

'Abby.' Pressing the intercom, she summoned the registrar from her break. 'We need you in Resus. Lavinia,' May ordered, 'take over the massage.'

He stood and watched, half heard May say to Abby something about James not feeling too good, but all he could really hear was the sound of gushing in his ears, and the blip, blip, blip of the cardiac monitor as Lavinia delivered cardiac massage.

Lorna's blouse was already undone, her bra cut and pushed to the side. Her boots or shoes had already been taken off, where they had attempted IV access. They were slicing through her soaked clothes with scissors, sheering through her torn stockings and underwear. He could see the scars from her operation and it made him want to weep, but instead he just stood there, watching them lift her pale knees and insert a catheter, knowing *how* much she would hate all this, tempted to tell them to just leave her alone, tempted to pick her up and run, but wanting them to carry on as well.

'Go to the on-call room,' May said to him. 'James, go to the on-call room, you look as if you're about to pass out.'

'I'm staying…'

He'd never felt more useless in his life. As an emergency consultant he was accustomed to crises, but to have her slam back into his life like this, he was literally paralysed. She was so white. Lorna had always been pale, yet now she was as white as the sheet she was lying on. Even her lips were white. The only colour on the bed was her hair, thick, long and red still, so she hadn't dyed it after all. In fact, she hadn't changed at all. This fragile, slender little thing was just as he remembered her, and the Lorna he'd known was such a private person she would loathe the intrusion on her body very much. The warming unit had been pushed aside as full access to her body was needed. Abby was here now, taking over, asking for peritoneal lavage—where a bag of warmed fluids would be run into her abdominal cavity. The anaesthetist called for an oesophageal warming tube, but then Abby checked the monitor, the fine VF required Lorna be defibrillated. As the first shock was delivered to the frail body, James truly thought he would vomit as her chest lifted off the resus bed.

She didn't deserve this!

May didn't just tell him to leave again, she took him. There were plenty of experienced staff in with the patient now and guiding him by the arm through the department as if he were sleep-walking, she took him into his office and sat him at his desk, where he put his head in his hands.

'Stay in there with her,' James said, hating being away yet knowing it was right that he was. There wasn't a hope in hell of being objective with her care. He'd never been able to be objective where Lorna was concerned, so how could he possibly start now? But the thought of her alone, the thought of him *not* being there for her when she needed him most, had him halting May as she turned to go. 'May, if they stop…'

'I'll come and get you.'

'Before they stop,' James added.

'Of course.'

'What's wrong with James?' Abby frowned, looking up briefly as May made her way back to the resuscitation area.

'He's been here since 3 a.m.,' May shrugged. She certainly wasn't going to fuel the fire! 'He mentioned he didn't feel well when we were waiting for the ambulance.'

There was no time to dwell on a consultant missing in action, though.

An hour in, May rang her husband and told him she'd be *really* late now and to go ahead and have dinner..

Very late, she told him a couple of hours later when she got the chance to ring again.

James had been right with his prediction—it was a long resuscitation.

The rapid warming did its job and then they had to work on getting the heart to beat independently, but for now she had an external pacemaker. Then there was a rapid CT scan, which showed a hairline fracture and cerebral swelling, and while all this was going on the police had tracked down her relatives and informed them of the direness of the situation.

'What do you think, Abby?' May asked as they walked back from ICU where the 'forgotten patient', as all the news channels were calling her now, lay fighting for her life, with many doctors and nurses fighting for it alongside her. But May had heard the consultant talking and could see it well enough herself. The outlook was dim.

'Well, she's been given every chance. And she did arrest at the scene, so that's something, but still it doesn't look at all good.' Abby said, her pretty face serious. 'Poor woman, she's my age, you know. Hopefully her parents will get here in time.'

'She could make it.' May said. 'We did get her back.'

'As what, though?' Abby said, stopping at a water fountain and filling a small cup with water. 'We've been going for hours, she's already got a head injury from the accident. I just wonder if we've done her any favours. Still…' She screwed her cup up and tossed it in the bin. 'At least her family might have a chance to say goodbye.'

And now May had to tell James.

The staff all thought he had gone home sick, so he hadn't been disturbed.

He was just as she'd left him, sitting at the desk with his head in his hands. He hadn't even turned on his desk light but the anguish in his face when he looked up to her would stay with May for ever.

'She's just been moved to ICU.' May dragged a chair over and sat beside him. 'She has some fractured ribs and a small hairline fracture to the skull, but…' James knew the score, but he still needed to hear it. 'She did make some movement when her temperature came up but Khan was worried she was about to convulse, so he's keeping her paralysed and intubated for forty-eight hours. She's had a CT, which shows cerebral swelling, but really…'

'We won't know for a while,' James finished for her.

'No, we won't. But, James…' She took his hand, because she cared about him, and because he really didn't need false hope, she made herself say it, 'It really is minute by minute at the moment. She's very unstable. Khan's not optimistic about her chances and neither is Abby. We're just hoping her parents get here soon. According to the papers in her car she was here in London for an interview. The police just contacted her next of kin—her parents. Apparently they're on their way.'

'Great!' There was a bitter note to his voice that May had never heard from James before.

'I'm sorry, James.' May patted his arm then rubbed it, hating to see him like this. 'You obviously know her.'

'I haven't seen her in ten years... I knew something was up, though not with her, of course, but since I got back from the accident...' His logical, analytical mind just tripped at that point. 'I knew something was wrong, I knew something wasn't right—it just doesn't make sense.'

'It does to me,' May said. 'How many times have we had babies brought in a whisper from death because their mums suddenly woke up to check them, or daughter who popped into their dad's for no real reason only to find him on the floor...'

'I just *knew* something was wrong.'

'And you were right,' May said, but she couldn't hold back any longer, she just had to know who this pale red-haired beauty was. 'Have you worked with her?' May asked, frowning because she would recognise most of the doctors who had been through the department and certainly Lorna, with her stunning hair, would have stood out, except May couldn't recall her at all.

'I knew her from medical school.'

'That's right—you went to medical school up in Scotland. Was she in your year?'

James shook his head. 'No, she was a couple of years below me.'

Even though he was sitting down he *still* looked as if he was about to pass out and May knew that Lorna must have been more to him that a fellow student a couple of years his junior. One of the downsides of working in Emergency was when friends or relatives came in unexpectedly, and she'd been on duty when James's own father had suffered a heart attack, yet still he had held it together that day.

He wasn't holding it together now.

'Did you used to go out with her?' May asked gently.

'A bit more than that.' James's voice was

suddenly urgent. 'I need to go and see her, before her parents get here.'

'Of course,' May said. 'I'll walk up to ICU with you.' Only she couldn't hold back the question that was on her mind any longer. They were just past the canteen and turning left for the lifts when May finally cracked and asked what she wanted to know. Yes, she was curious, but it wasn't just that that had her probing. She wanted to help James just as she did with any friend or relative of a critically ill patient—and to do that, it would help to know.

'Who is she, James?'

It took till they were in the lift and heading upwards toward ICU for James to answer.

'She's my ex-wife.'

CHAPTER THREE

MAY HADN'T SEEN that one coming. Oh, she knew they all had pasts but she'd been working with James since he'd come to the department on his emergency rotation as a senior house officer, had known him since he'd been fresh faced out of his internship, yet never once had he mentioned that he was or had been married.

For James, that walk to ICU was the longest of his life. Stuck in his office these past few hours, he'd almost prepared himself for her death. He had tried not to think of what would be going on in the resuscitation room. He had just thought about her and felt strangely grateful that Lorna was here in London, that he could be with her now if that door opened and May told him they were stopping the resuscitation attempt.

Yet she'd made it through that, and now he must make it through this.

It felt strange to buzz the intercom and ask for permission to enter, only not as a doctor this time, to have to wash his hands and sit in a little side room as May spoke with the nursing staff.

'They're just settling her in.' May clucked like an old hen when she returned, pouring him a cup of water from the little sink in the relatives' room. 'You'll need to turn off your mobile here, before you go in.'

He pulled it out, saw that there were eight missed calls and he hadn't even heard the phone ring.

Ellie. He glanced at the clock on the wall. He was supposed to have been there hours ago. He turned off his phone and used the one on the table beside him, listening to it ring and her irritated voice when she realised who it was.

'Hi, Ellie.' He tried to keep his voice vaguely

normal. 'Look, obviously I'm not going to be able to make it tonight.' He heard her strained sigh and glanced up at May, who was pretending not to listen. 'No, it's not work…' He raked a hand through his hair, took a breath and continued, 'You know I told you about Lorna…' His words were met with silence. 'Well, she's had an accident. She's here at the hospital in Intensive Care. There's no one else here for her yet.'

He glanced over to May, who must have read the 'Please Wash Your Hands' sign about twenty times now.

'No.' James said, and then 'No,' again. 'Look I'd really rather just deal with this on my own. I'll call you tomorrow.'

'Ellie.' James said, when May sat down.

'Your girlfriend?' May asked, because even though she never usually would, she was here tonight as a friend and colleague and she was also treating him as a relative of a patient, trying to piece it all together so that she could help him best. 'So she knows about Lorna.'

'I told Ellie about Lorna a couple of months ago. We were starting to get a bit more serious. I thought it was right…' His voice trailed off.

'You were married to Lorna?' May checked. 'For how long?'

'Not even a year.' He could have stopped there. A year wasn't long after all and it had been a decade ago. It should all be neatly relegated to the past, only he'd never quite managed to do that, had never been able to add a neat full stop to that chapter in his life and move on. He'd tried, though, over and over he'd tried, but that year with Lorna had been a rollercoaster ride from start to finish and he felt as if he were back on it again. He'd wondered sometimes at the ease with which patients gave the most personal details, had decided there was this need to make sense of the life the doctors and nurses were fighting for, to make that person real and warm and perhaps, a need to put things into frantic perspective. He had been right, because here he was doing the same now, trying to match up that limp lifeless patient with the person he knew or, rather, had known.

'She was a couple of years younger than me,' James explained. 'She seemed a strange little thing, very prim and shockable, or she was when we were at medical school. She never came to many of the social things, but she always stood out.'

'With her hair?' May smiled, but James shook his head.

'There are plenty of redheads in Scotland. I don't know May, she just always stood out for me, sort of stood apart. I was a bit fascinated by her, I guess. And then one night there was a party and she was there…' He even smiled at the memory, his face ashen but still he smiled in recall. 'She just blew me away, we couldn't stop talking. We'd known each other vaguely for a while yet that night it was as if we'd met each other for the first time. We went to bed that night. She'd never slept with anyone before…' He shook his head as if he still couldn't believe what had happened. 'But there was no question in my mind that she'd ever sleep with anyone but me again. I was crazy about her. We spent the next two weeks in bed, not just that, talking, studying, May it was the best two weeks of my life. It was crazy, it was wild, but it made perfect sense at the time.'

'And then what?'

James didn't answer straight away. He stared up at the clock that must surely have stopped, because if felt as if they'd been sitting in there for hours. Felt as if he was living it again after all these years.

'Let's just find out!' Normally calm and practical, he needed to be even more so here, James had realised, because Lorna was a mess. Handing her the little paper bag with the pregnancy test kit he had bought, he remembered guiding her to the bathroom, but at the door she baulked.

'You don't understand…'

'Lorna!' He was getting exasperated now. For

two days she'd been panicking that her period was late, two days of anguish, which, over and over he had pointed out, might be unnecessary—they had been careful. 'Let's just find out first if there really is anything to worry about.'

He'd sounded so calm and practical, but sitting outside the bathroom in his junior doctors residence flat, he had been nervous. He'd just started his internship, had just moved out of student accommodation, and was finally starting to earn some money—and now this! As careful as they had been...well, they'd barely been out of bed, and... He closed his eyes and blew out a breath, trying not to think about how they could have been a bit more careful. Well, they would be in the future, James had decided. She hadn't wanted to go on the Pill in case her parents found out, which James had found bizarre! Well, they'd have to sort something out, they couldn't go through this each month.

They wouldn't have to.

Her sobs from the bathroom told James before

he even went in that there would be no second chances. Holding her sobbing body, he tried to comfort her, to tell her it would be okay, that they would sort something out, that they would get through this, only she was beyond comfort.

And as he held her late into the night, only then did the realisation hit that she wasn't worried about her career, or her future, or how a baby would affect her life, and she wasn't worried what a pregnancy three weeks into a relationship might do to them. The only thing that consumed her, the only thing that seemed to literally terrify her, was how her father would react.

'What happened then, James?' May's voice broke him from his introspection.

'We found out that she was pregnant.'

'Hello!' A bubbly ICU nurse who introduced herself as Angela came in and interrupted them, but even with her bright demeanour James could tell she was nervous—it was never easy dealing with staff, especially when the patient was so ill.

'Sorry to have kept you waiting so long, but we're still having a lot of trouble stabilising her. Now, I just need to go through a few details. You're Lorna's ex-husband?' she checked.

'That's right.'

'Firstly, is there any past history you're aware of that we should know about?'

James hesitated for a second, not sure it was relevant, not really wanting to share that part of his past, but if it helped her, they had to hear it.

'I don't think so. She had an appendectomy when she was twelve, I believe, and she had an an ectopic pregnancy, but that was ages ago.'

'How long?' Angela asked, scribbling the information down.

'Ten, nearly eleven years ago.'

'Anything else? Diabetes, epilepsy…'

James shook his head. 'Not that I'm aware of.'

'Do you keep in contact with Lorna?'

'No.'

'And how long is it since you've spoken with her?'

James gave a tight swallow. 'Ten years.'

'I see.' James felt sorry for Angela, it was a difficult situation after all. He had no real right to see Lorna, less right even than a person on the street who might walk in now and claim to know her. Divorce did that, James had long ago realised. 'Her family are on their way,' Angela said. 'They should be landing any time now—they got a flight as soon as they were informed. Obviously, while Lorna is unable to speak for herself, wc havc to rcly on the next of kin to determine her wishes, which in this case is her parents.'

'They won't be thrilled to see me!' James looked her right in the eye. 'Look, there was nothing acrimonious in the divorce.' It was killing him to discuss this with a stranger, he *wouldn't* discuss this with a stranger. 'It just didn't work out, but we did both care about each other. I know I'm her ex, which should mean I'm the last person she wants to see,' he faltered, because from previous indication that was exactly the case.

'She was in full cardiac arrest in my department. I just need to see for myself…'

'I understand.' Angela said, but James was quite sure she didn't. However, her eyes were kind and she gave a sort of half-smile. Then what she said next made him realise that maybe she did understand after all. 'I'm divorced myself, but I know I'd want to see him if he was so ill. But once the family get here, the decision will be theirs.'

'I understand that.' James gave a grateful nod. 'I'm not going to get in the way.'

'Do you want me to come?' May offered, but James shook his head. 'I'll just wait here.'

He'd always wished for one more chance to see her, to talk to her, to say he was sorry, so very sorry for all that had happened and to find out why, and some of his wishes had been granted tonight. Even though they hurt like hell, he was incredibly grateful for them.

She was pinker now. It was the first thing he noticed when he approached, just as if she were sleeping really, apart from the tubes everywhere.

The warming unit was on—a large inflated duvet, that would help maintain her temperature, and she looked tiny beneath it with just her head and shoulders visible.

He'd wanted this moment with her, would have pulled rank or just stormed his way in to get it, only now it was here, James didn't know what to do, didn't know what she'd want him to do.

A chair had been placed by the bed so he perched on it. Angela took over from the float nurse who had been watching Lorna and now she sat, high up on a stool at the end of the bed, reading all the equipment and filling in the charts, watching Lorna every second, which was what Intensive Care was, after all, but he'd have killed for just a couple of minutes alone with her.

'She's the most private person.' James glanced over at Angela. 'I mean, she'd really hate all this. I know anyone would, but…' He was rambling, really didn't know what to do. Her collar bones were exposed so he pulled the warming unit up higher around her neck. She'd always been slim but she was skinny now. As Angela exposed her arms to check her reflexes he could see the veins, see her neat, short nails which, unlike her toes, were left unpolished.

'Here.' Angela left one skinny forearm out from under the warming unit. "Why don't you hold her hand, tell her that you're here? It might be reassuring for her to hear a familiar voice.' He hadn't held Lorna's hand in ten years and he didn't know if he should, but when he did her hand felt cool, but that was how she had always felt. He stared at the bony fingers and the blue veins on the back of her hand and the smattering of freckles that he had adored but she had so hated.

'She was always cold.' He was talking to Angela but looking at Lorna. 'She'd come in after a night shift and she'd be frozen.' Now he was remembering things that he had chosen not to, those freezing winter mornings when she'd climb into bed beside him as cold as the ice outside, or when he'd crawl into bed beside her at 7 a.m., cold himself to find her for once warm. He wanted to warm her now, wanted to crawl into bed and hold her, *feel* her again. Only he couldn't, hadn't been able to for a decade now.

What to do, what to do? His head was spinning. She'd left him, would she even want him sitting beside her now?

Yes.

Accidents did happen—James Morrell knew that better than anyone, but for her to be here when she was so very ill… His head tightened at the thought that she might die, or be brain damaged, but somehow there must be a reason that she was here. Somehow she had come back to him, even if it was just to say goodbye.

He was holding her hand to his face now and it was like a dam breaking. Feeling her skin beneath his lips he leant over, buried his face in her hair, inhaled the last wisps of the lavender shampoo she had always used, felt her cheekbone rest beneath his.

For a second he thought someone must have

died in the next bed, because he could hear crying—a deep, pained crying. It was only when he felt a hand on his shoulder that James realised it was him.

'Talk to her, James.' Angela must have gone and got May, because it was her at his shoulder, urging him to say what he had to while he had this chance. So he did—told Lorna all the things he'd wanted to say, all the things he never had, told her over and over in the pathetic hope that maybe she could hear him.

'Her family just arrived.' Ages later, but way too soon, May prompted him to move. 'They've asked that you leave.'

He'd worked in Emergency for years and had never understood it—those flashpoint rows that were so out of place in a hospital, rows that infuriated the staff and prompted review panels to be set up to avoid them. But seeing that smug face come towards him, seeing the beatific smile of Minister McClelland as he approached him, suddenly James understood.

'James.' Minister McClelland held out his hand. 'Thank you for sitting with Lorna till we arrived. It is much appreciated.'

James knew that he should nod, shake his hand, take his exit cue and just leave, except he couldn't.

'Of course I sat with her.'

'James!' How did one smile and shoot venom at the same time, but Minister McClelland had it down to a fine art. 'It was very kind of you to take time out of your schedule—'

'What do you mean " take time"?' James interrupted. 'She was my wife.'

"Now your ex-wife,' Minister McClelland neatly pointed out. 'She left you, remember?' He wasn't smiling now, just dripping false compassion. 'Lorna divorced you more than ten years ago. As I said, Betty and I have drawn a lot of comfort knowing that someone who used to be close to our daughter could sit with her till we arrived. But we're here now—and we'd like you to leave.'

'Lorna would want—'

'I know what my daughter would want, James.' Minister McClelland broke in. 'You haven't seen her in years. She's a very different woman to the one you took advantage of then—and, I can assure you, the woman Lorna is now would not want you sitting by her bedside. Now, you've caused my family enough pain in the past, you'll forgive me if I don't invite it in again.'

He headed to his daughter's bedside and James stood there, knowing he had to leave, but loath to.

'Come on, James.' It was close to midnight, but that wasn't why May was in a hurry, she just wanted James away from the toxic atmosphere the minister had created. 'You've seen her, you've spoken to her.' And with that he had to be content.

'Thanks for all you did,' James said to Angela, and took a long, last, lingering look at Lorna. 'Will you call me if there is any change? I'll be staying at the hospital.'

'Her family have asked that only they be given information as to her condition.'

Bastard. The word hissed in his head.

'There's a lot of press interest and things— they've made their wishes very clear.'

Oh, they'd always made their wishes very clear. He could see them all praying around her now and wondered what Lorna would want him to do, only he truly didn't know. Out of control and hating it, he asserted himself as best he could. 'Well, I'm not asking as the press and I'm not asking as her ex-husband. I am the emergency consultant—and she did come through my department. I have every right to be informed if our prolonged resuscitation was successful. Page me when there's any change either way.'

'Certainly, Dr. Morrell.'

'Mr Morrell,' James corrected, and then he gave her a small smile. 'Again, thanks for your help.'

CHAPTER FOUR

ICU *DID* keep James informed of Lorna's progress.

Despite Ellie's protests that she was hardly seeing him, he moved into the on-call room and divided his time between work, of which there was plenty, and staring at the ceiling, or dozing on the small single bed, jerking into consciousness whenever his phone bleeped.

Sixty hours later, after two failed attempts, she was successfully extubated and twenty-four hours after that on the Tuesday morning she was transferred from ICU to a medical ward. This was all extremely encouraging, except Lorna's consciousness levels were variable and at best she was disorientated and confused, at worst she didn't know her own name.

May never said a word to anyone, but the hospital world was a small one and word soon spread that the dashing but elusive Mr Morrell's ex-wife was a patient and that he was *devastated* apparently—absolutely *devastated*.

Which he wasn't. Apart from the shock of seeing her and the hellish hours waiting to see whether she lived or died, apart from that one breakdown when he'd held her again after all those years, James was doing fine.

'I'm fine,' he said in answer to everyone who enquired.

'I'm fine,' he said to Ellie when she asked why he hadn't called, and why he wouldn't talk to her about it. He was just busy, that was all.

'Look, really I'm fine,' he said to Abby, when she said she *knew* what he was going through and when it hit him, as it surely would, she was there if he needed to talk.

'Fine,' he said to Minister McClelland when

a week after the accident Lorna's father came to speak with James, who was going through the medial roster and having an impromptu meeting with May at the nursing station about the increasing pressure the shortage of doctors was creating for the staff.

Naturally, May stood to excuse herself and James asked if she'd mind waiting for the whole sixty seconds that this would take.

'We'd like to thank you and your team.' The minister shook James's hand and for James it was as if he was touching a snake. 'Betty and I are leaving for Scotland today, now that we know Lorna's on the mend. We have the major fundraiser for the church this weekend and I want to thank my congregation properly for all their prayers and, of course…' he cocked his head to the side just as he always did when he tried to inject a little humour into his preaching '…I'd like to properly thank the man himself.'

Did he think he was the only one who had prayed for her? James had been on his knees that night, had prayed like he never had in his life—not, James realised, that his prayers counted for much in the minister's eyes.

'Have a safe trip.' James said, then picked up his pen to resume working. He had nothing to say to the man—well, that wasn't strictly true, he had *plenty* that he could say, but he refused to go there.

'There is one other thing.' James gritted his teeth as Minister McClelland put on his serious expression and James knew what was coming next. Strange how the Scottish lilt he had found so endearing in Lorna grated when it came from her father. 'As I'm sure you will understand, Lorna's feeling extremely uncomfortable.'

'Well.' James deliberately didn't get the point. 'It's early days yet, but if her pain control is proving a problem, I can have a word.'

'Not about that,' Minister McClelland snapped as James suppressed a smile. 'She's extremely uncomfortable knowing that she's in the same hospital as you.'

'Really?' James raised his eyebrows, but inside he rallied a touch. She must have improved considerably since he'd spoken to the ward if she knew that she was in the same hospital he worked in. Till a couple of days ago she had been having trouble with her own name.

'Lorna's quite clear on the matter—she doesn't want you coming to see her.'

'I haven't *been* to see her.' James pointed out.

'Yes, but now that we are going back to Scotland, we want to make sure that that continues.' Now you're not guarding her bed James wanted to say, but didn't. 'It took a long time for Lorna to get over things,' Minister McClelland explained. 'A long time, but now she's got her life together, she's seeing a nice young fellow, he's a doctor actually, he's working in Kenya at the moment.'

'Good for Lorna!'

'You staying away is what's good for Lorna.' He stood up and offered his hand, but James refused to take it. There was no need for feigned politeness now, no need for anything really—the McClellands were all a part of his past. As the minister went to go, he spelt it out one final time. 'What I'm saying, James, is that if you do have Lorna's interests at heart, it would be better if you stay away. You are not to go near my daughter.'

'Fine.' For maybe the fiftieth time that morning, James said it. He was speaking to the minister's back as he walked out.

'He's a charmer!' May didn't even pretend that she hadn't heard anything this time.

'He always was!" James attempted a shrug, but his shoulders were so rigid with tension that they barely moved. 'Funny how nothing changes.'

'Are you going to go and see her,' May pushed, 'now that her parents are gone?'

'No.' He'd made up his mind and Minister McClelland had neatly affirmed it. 'There's no point raking up the past.'

'Oh, I think it's already been well and truly tilled and turned. Let's have a coffee, James.'

May wasn't asking him, she was telling him. 'In your office!'

'Just leave it, May.' He *had* gone to his office, because *this* he certainly wasn't going to do on the shop floor—his personal life had already provided enough entertainment for the entire hospital these past days. From professor to porter, everyone seemed to be offering sympathetic smiles, or stopped talking when he walked in, and James didn't like it one bit. He certainly wasn't going to go up to the ward just to add to the drama of it all. 'It was over years ago between Lorna and me. You've heard what Minister McClelland said—she's uncomfortable that I'm here and she doesn't want me to come and see her.'

'According to her father.' May said. 'James, you *were* devastated when she was brought in.'

'It was a shock.' James shrugged. 'She was my wife once—I'm not that callous.'

'You're not callous at all! You married her because she was pregnant, I take it.'

He gave a curt nod.

'And then she lost the baby.'

'Yep!' His voice was flip, but there was a muscle pounding in his cheek and finally he relented a touch. 'Lorna went crazy when she found out she was pregnant—she said her father would be wild, I told her that he'd come round, that once the news sank in, he'd support her.'

'She didn't consider an abortion?'

'Nope.' James shook his head. 'Not for a minute. I said I'd support her in any way I could. I went with her to tell her family… May, I have never seen anything like that man's reaction. The names he called her, called me. He wasn't worried about Lorna, about her future, he was worried what his congregation would say—what people would think. We were married two weeks later and it still wasn't enough. We had to keep the pregnancy quiet. He didn't want people counting on their fingers and working out dates—we moved down to London just to get away.'

'Oh, James.' May shook her head at the horror of it all. 'I know…'

'No, May, you don't know.' James said angrily. 'You don't know what he's like.'

'Actually, James, I do.' May stood her ground. 'I worked for ten years on a gynaecological ward. I didn't actually like working there, but I'd laid out two beautiful young women's bodies in my training. Beautiful women, who were too scared to tell their parents they were pregnant. I chose to do the best job I could on that gynae ward for the sake of those young girls. So don't stand there and tell me I don't know, because I do.'

And James understood that she did, wished for a moment that he'd spoken to her about it years ago. In those early days when he'd started at the hospital, he'd been so blind with confusion and grief he'd been positive no one would understand—yet he'd been working all the time, next to one woman who perhaps did. 'At her antenatal we found out the baby was ectopic, she had to go to Theatre straight away. It had already ruptured by the time she got there. I rang her father to tell him, and all he was was relieved. He didn't say it out loud, but I knew from his voice he was relieved that his congregation wouldn't be counting backwards on their fingers now when the baby arrived. There would be plenty of time for other babies apparently and he and his wife said the same when they came to see Lorna.'

'She wanted that one,' May offered but James shook his head.

'We both wanted that one,' he corrected her.

'I'm sorry.' May nodded.

'It was a shock finding out she was pregnant, but we'd dealt with that. We got married and even if it was rushed, even if we were broke and the timing could have been better, we were crazy about each other and looking forward to being parents. When we lost the baby, we lost everything, May. She walked out on the marriage before the first anniversary, headed off back to Scotland and became a GP, refused to even talk to me. It's taken me years to get over what happened and finally I have. I've been seeing Ellie for more than a year now. That's the longest relationship I've had since Lorna and if you think I'm going to jeopardise it by heading up there to go over old times you're wrong. For a start, it wouldn't be fair on Ellie.'

'It's not fair on Ellie if your heart's elsewhere,' May said. 'Maybe it's time to find out. Maybe you'll see Lorna and feel nothing and you can move on properly, because it sounds to me like you haven't.'

'Oh, and you'd know, would you?' James said, annoyed with May for saying out loud what he had been thinking. 'You've been married for forty-two years—'

'Which makes me an expert!' May answer tartly. 'Because you don't stay married for forty-two years these days without learning a thing or two! Do you want me to go and speak to her?'

'And say what?' When May widened her eyes

a touch, even James managed a reluctant smile—May was certainly never lost for words and, in her line of work, had handled far more than this little drama without rehearsal. 'Okay, okay,' he said, irritated but curious and just a little bit relieved too that he might hear what Lorna had to say. 'Go and test the water.'

Lorna remembered virtually nothing of ICU. Just the odd blurry memory of noise and someone asking her to say her name and if she knew where she was and then being wheeled through the hospital.

There had been lots of lights flashing into her eyes and people asking her what her name was and even though she'd known it, she hadn't known how to say it, her mouth and tongue refusing to obey. She had just wanted them to leave her alone so that she could go back to sleep, because it had hurt to be awake. It felt as if a bus had been parked on her chest and moving her limbs in response to the questions had taken a massive effort and one she hadn't had the energy for.

'Come on.' Someone was pinching her ear. 'Tell me your name.'

'Lorna.'

'And do you know where you are, Lorna?' It was a very good question and one that had been asked a few times, Lorna hazily recalled.

'Lorna, answer the nurse!' Dad was there, which didn't exactly cheer her up. Here she was in hospital and her dad still managed to make her feel as if she was misbehaving. Oh, yes, that was where she was...

'Hospital.' She managed a groggy answer through cracked, swollen lips, peeled her eyes open a fraction as the nurse demanded she do so.

'That's right. Now, can you give my hands a squeeze? Come on, nice and tight.' The nurse was chatting away. 'You had an accident, Lorna. Do you remember anything.' She didn't remember anything so instead of answering she tried to go back to sleep—she was just sick of the intrusion. Over and over they asked the same thing. 'You had a car crash and now you're in North London Regional Hospital.'

'No.' She shook her head because *that* was impossible. Little flashes of memory darted in, as if she was trying to recall a dream. She'd had interviews in London, that much made sense, but she definitely hadn't applied for a job at North London Regional Hospital. Even though they'd advertised positions, she had deliberately avoided the hospital because that was where James was working.

She knew because she had checked.

'No,' Lorna said, too exhausted to argue, choosing instead to go back to sleep.

She'd lay in a sort of suspended existence for the next couple of days, not examining why she was here or what was wrong, coming back to the world in stages, accepting now rather than arguing, existing rather than living.

Her mother had gone to the shops and bought

her several of the most disgusting pairs of nylon pyjamas, a nylon dressing gown and a pair of old men's slippers, which hopefully had rubber soles because the static energy she gave off when the nurse for the first time wheeled her to the bathroom and helped her shower and dress could have powered a small nation.

And maybe a day or two later, while dozing, she heard them discussing the expense of staying in London, how she was clearly going to be here for a while. It had taken a moment to work out that the *she* they were referring to was her.

'We just left everything and dashed down when we heard what had happened,' her mother said the next morning as she fed Lorna warm tea through a straw. 'The neighbours are feeding the pets, I haven't got any clothes. We don't want you to think we're abandoning you. If you give me the key to Grace's I'll sort out some clothes and toiletries, it will be nice to have your own things'

'Thanks.'

'It's just we've been here a week now.'

'A week?' Lorna halted herself then, knew her endless questions just upset her mother and exasperated her father, but *a week?* She felt as if it should be two, maybe four days at the most.

'You do understand.' Betty had hugged her gently so as not to hurt her sore chest. 'Only the doctor says you could be in for a while yet and we struggled to get a minister last Sunday to cover your father…'

'Mum, you've done enough already, both of you.' She lay back on the pillow, exhausted, even though it was only eight-thirty in the morning. 'I'm so sorry for all the trouble.'

'These things are sent to try us!' her father said, giving her a rather wintry smile. 'We'll ring when we get home.'

How, Lorna tried to fathom, could he always make her feel guilty? He could make her feel like a troublesome child with one look, even at thirty-two years of age. She could feel the tension start to seep out of the room as the door closed. Despite drifting in and out of consciousness, she had seen more of her parents these past few days that she had in ages, just concentrated time, with no nieces or nephews to distract, no parishioners dropping in. Just the three of them stuck in this blessed room and James Morrell, as she had found out, on the loose in the building!

'Hello, there!' A kind, lined face, speaking in a thick Dublin accent, walked towards her and with a small smile Lorna held out her arm for her blood pressure to be taken. 'Lorna McClelland, and I'm in North London Regional Hospital.'

'So you are.' The nurse smiled. 'Only I'm not here to do your obs. I'm May Donnelly. I was working in Emergency when you were brought in. I've just come to see how you're getting on.'

'I'm sorry!' Embarrassed, Lorna winced. 'Believe it or not, I was making a joke. I couldn't remember my own name for the first couple of days, let alone tell them where I was.'

'I'm not surprised!' May perched on the edge of the bed and Lorna moved her knees. 'You gave us quite a fright.'

'I've given everyone a fright!' Lorna sighed. 'My parents just went home.'

'Good or bad?' May asked, and there was something about her eyes, something so knowing in that question, that Lorna felt relief. Tears welled in her eyes for the first time since the accident.

'I've just caused so much trouble…'

'Accidents do that.' May patted her arm. 'But it's not you causing the trouble.'

'You don't know them.'

'No,' May said gently. 'But I did meet them on the night of your accident.'

'Oh.'

'I was with James when he came up to Intensive Care to see you.'

She couldn't even manage an 'oh'.

So he had been to see her. Her parents hadn't told her that. Her father had said he'd had a brief discussion with James, who of course had wanted to check that she was recovering, but that James had felt it better if he didn't come to see her.

'He was the doctor in charge when you were brought in.' May let the words sink in and it took a while. Lorna closed her eyes as she tried, and failed, to comprehend how it must have been for him. They may only have been married a short while, but she couldn't fathom her own response if she'd been on duty and it had been James who'd been brought in critically ill.

'Did he tell you?' Lorna asked. 'Do you know that we…?' Her voice trailed off, but May nodded.

'I only found out that he'd been married that evening.'

'How was he? How was he when he realised it was me?'

'That would be telling tales out of school,' May said, 'but naturally he was upset. He's asked me to come up and see you.' Those tears were welling but Lorna sniffed them back. It hurt that he was still so bitter or, worse, blasé, that he couldn't even come and check on her himself, hurt more than it rightly should. Only May hadn't finished. 'He was hoping to come up and see you himself, but he didn't want to, if it might upset you further.'

'No.' Lorna shook her head. 'I don't know. I thought he might have come up already.'

'He would have, except…' May gave her arm a little squeeze '…it might have been hard on you, with your parents here and everything.'

'Did Dad tell him not to?' May didn't answer. 'Ask him since when he listened to my father?' And they came then, the tears she'd been holding back since her eyes had opened in ICU. It was the sheer horror of waking up sore and bruised and not knowing where she was and finding out her parents were here and that James was too. It wasn't just a car that had crashed that day, her whole world had. If May had pressed a tissue in her hand and told her to calm down it would have been better, but instead she was stroking her hair and patiently telling her to let it out. 'You have a good cry, pet.' So Lorna did, for the first time since she had awoken to this strange, confusing world. When she had finished and May asked if there was anything she could do for her, Lorna felt so much better she was tempted to ask if May didn't mind going to buy some decent pyjamas for her, but thought that might be pushing it.

'I'll let him know you'll see him.'

It wasn't exactly the look one hoped for when you had to meet one's ex, Lorna thought, wishing she had the energy to drag a comb through her hair and trying frantically not to think of the bigger picture, wondering what he'd look like, what they'd say to each other, what she'd say to him if he asked why she'd walked out on him all those years ago.

But nothing, not an hour lying thinking about it and racking her brains as to how she would feel, came close to the sweep of emotion as he pushed open the door and for the first time in a decade she came face to face with him.

'Lorna…'

She couldn't speak, just had no idea what to say as he stood there. His voice was just as deep, his shoulders just as broad, his eyes just as green. She'd thought she'd finished crying with that nice Irish nurse, but the second he walked into the room Lorna started again.

Ten years of pain came bubbling to the surface as the man she loved, the man she had always loved, walked towards her once more.

CHAPTER FIVE

HE'D had no idea what he would say, or do. He didn't know if he was angry, bitter, hurt, or simply no longer cared any more. Very deliberately James hadn't examined those feelings in years and certainly he'd tried not to these past few days. But seeing the way the tip of her nose went red, just as it had back then, seeing those huge amber eyes well the second he walked into the room, seeing the black, swollen eyelids and the glimpse of her badly bruised chest peeking out from her pyjamas and hearing her sob, knowing all she had just been through—it was entirely right that gently, very gently, he took her in his arms.

How could he not?

'It's okay, you're okay…' He said it over and over, to himself not just to her. He held her and breathed her in, because the last time he'd held her he'd thought she must die or, worse, live with a mind that wasn't hers. He let her go only when the nurse came in to do her obs. He watched Lorna blink as she correctly stated where she was but she faltered on the date.

'Do you know what day it is?'

'Wednesday…' Lorna blinked. 'I mean…' She shook her head.

'It's Friday,' the nurse said. 'Don't worry Lorna, it will all come back. Do you need anything?'

'Just some water, please.' James frowned at the full jug and tumbler on the table beside them, wondering why she didn't get it herself, but he watched as the nurse poured her a drink and peeled open a straw, holding the cup for Lorna, who took a couple of sips.

Only then did James realise just how fragile she was.

'My hands.' Lorna explained a bit sheepishly. 'They're still a bit numb, I keep dropping things.'

'You'll get there.'

'So everyone keeps saying.'

'So how are you?' James asked once they were alone.

'Not bad, considering.'

'Considering what?' James asked shrewdly, seeing the nervous dart of her eyes as he gently confronted her. 'How are you really?'

'Scared.' Lorna admitted it for the first time. Not wanting to create waves while her parents had been there, she'd been the model patient, had tried to answer all their questions without asking any of her own, but somehow to James she could admit the truth. 'I don't actually know what I'm doing here.'

'Has anyone told you what happened?'

'I don't know.' He could see the terror in her eyes. Her voice was still hoarse from the endotracheal tube and no matter how much of an improvement there was, he was reminded, if he needed it, just how very ill she had been recently. 'I mean, I know there was a car accident, I know I was in London for some job interviews, I just don't understand what's happened to me. I didn't want to worry my parents by telling them how confused I am. I feel like I've missed the start of a film and I can't ask anyone to explain. I don't even know what day it is till someone tells me.'

'Hey.' This he *could* deal with. In this case he did know what to do. 'You've been so ill, Lorna. Just three days ago you were in Intensive Care. It's normal *not* to be able to remember things.'

'Not as badly as this—'

'Yes.' James interrupted. 'Yes, Lorna. The fact we're even having this conversation shows you've got insight. That's good.'

'I guess.' She let his word soothe her, lay back on the pillows and closed her eyes for a moment.

'Do you want me to fill you in?' James saw her frown and because it was Lorna, even with a head injury, he knew what she was thinking. 'I meant fill you in on the last week.' He watched a smile lift the edges of her pale lips as he continued, 'Not the last decade!'

'Please, then.'

'Do you want me to write it down?' He smiled a touch when she gave a small giggle.

'Just tell me and if I've forgotten again by the time you go then, yes, write it down.'

'You did have a car accident, there was a coach crash on the M1, you do have a head injury, but from all the reports it's slight.'

'But I was unconscious for hours, Mum said, before they found me.'

'No. Do you keep a blanket in the car?' She frowned and nodded.

'On the back seat. There's a tear…'

'Well, you were wrapped in it when they found you so you must have come to at some point and had the ability to know you were cold and needed to get warm. Lorna, it took them a long time to find your car.' He couldn't stand to think of what she'd been through. Maybe it was better if she didn't remember it, but James realised she had to know the truth. 'It was four or so hours before your car was found. You'd veered to avoid the collision apparently—and you lost control. In all the chaos of the major incident your car wasn't noticed till the clear-up.'

There was a tiny chirrup, like a bird singing that she couldn't see but could picture, an image flitting into her mind of trying to get her phone but not being able to reach to the floor of the car, her head a lead weight against the headrest, snow billowing in through the smashed wind-screen. Inching her arm around the twisted seat, it had taken for ever, but she had reached the blanket, she *had* known to stay warm.

'You've been through an awful lot, but you're coming out of it now.' James said assuredly. 'You really are doing marvellously.'

'Really?'

'Really.' James nodded. 'You'll soon be back to the old Lorna.' He gave a small swallow, as he remembered the Lorna of old. 'Okay, I'd better get down to the department now.'

'You're a consultant?'

'Yes.'

'You always said that's what you wanted to do.'

Oh, there had been a lot of things he'd wanted, but James just smiled, wished her well again and deliberately didn't kiss her on the cheek.

'Are you on over the weekend?'

'Not officially. I'll be called in a couple of times no doubt.'

'Well, if you are, it would be nice if you could stop by.'

He gave a small nod that didn't say yes and didn't say no—more a *we'll see*—and she lay watching the door long after he'd gone, soothed by his visit but unsettled all the same. She should never have asked him to come and visit her. Lorna turned and stared at the now familiar sight of the hospital generator. She was depleted completely by the morning's events, not even turning her head when the nurse came in and changed the rate on her IV. Instead, the little energy Lorna had left was all being concentrated on James.

Stay away, she willed him. Even though she wanted him to come and visit, for his sake she hoped that he didn't.

For James's sake, she truly hoped that he'd stay away.

CHAPTER SIX

'HERE.' James put down his pager and keys and placed a large take-out coffee in front of Lorna and started to peel a straw from its wrapper, but she stopped him.

'I'm doing better.' She smiled, taking a sip of decent coffee and relishing it for a moment before continuing. 'And I am *not* drinking coffee through a straw.'

She *was* doing better. Since her parents had gone and James had explained things, the mist seemed to be clearing a touch. Lorna had chatted with the nurses, even walked the length of the ward a couple of times, shuffling along as the nurse had pushed her drip, but it felt good to be up and about, and it felt even better to see James again.

'May said you were on duty when I came in.' Her eyes met his, knew, despite all that had happened between them, how appalling that must have been. 'I'm so sorry for that.'

'It's hardly your fault. Still, it never entered my head it might be you when the ambulance doors opened—I never thought I'd see you here. So how come you were looking for a job in London?'

'I had four interviews lined up.' As she told him, she was remembering things herself.

'So you're moving back here?'

'If I get one of the jobs…'

'I thought you hated London, you said you weren't happy—' He stopped himself then. Now was surely not the time to examine their past.

'It wasn't the place,' Lorna said quietly, which could only mean that it had been their relationship that she'd hated, or him. 'I've been working as a GP, and I've also been doing some cover at one of the cottage hospitals. I just wanted a change—I really liked working in a big city hospital.'

'They have them in Scotland,' James pointed out.

'I just…' She shook her head, just wouldn't go there with him. 'I just wanted a change. I handed in my notice last month, and I thought I'd have no trouble getting a job, but the interviews didn't go too well. I think they look at the patient numbers I'm used to dealing with and think I'm not equipped to cope. They don't seem to want to understand that often I'm the only doctor around for miles—they don't seem to comprehend the scope of things I have to deal with.'

'You should have called me.' James gave a half-smile. 'I could have put in a word.'

'I almost wish I had.' There was a small rueful smile on her lips. 'So now I'm jobless, homeless, and my car's a write-off.'

'Homeless?' James frowned.

'I put my flat on the market ages ago. It sold really suddenly, but they wanted a quick settlement, so it was either lose the sale or get out. I'm staying at a friend's. She's on holiday at the moment so I'm house-sitting. It was only supposed to be for a couple of weeks, that's why I had so many interviews lined up.'

'Well, you're a guest of North London Regional Hospital for the next week or so.' James smiled. 'Who knows? They might give you a job offer.'

She fiddled with his keyring for something to do, saw, then felt the weight of a big silver 'L' that hung from it.

'Not you.' James smiled, noticing her noticing the key ring. 'I'm not that much of a sad case.'

'I know.' She put down his keys, flushed just a touch at the edge in his voice and knew he was telling the truth. 'James, I hate to ask a favour. I did ask my mum but she came back from the shop with the wrong one. Do you think—if you get a chance, I mean—you could buy me a phone charger?'

'Sure.' He rummaged in her drawer and found her phone then wrote down the model number. 'It won't be till tomorrow, though, I've got a list of things to do today and then I've got a wedding reception to go to tonight.'

'That will be nice.' She stopped as he pulled a face. 'You're not looking forward to it, then.'

'It's Ellie's cousin. He's a real pain, neither of us want to go.'

'Ellie?'

'My girlfriend.' James said, walking over to the window and staring out at the hospital generator, billowing smoke into the cold grey sky as Lorna leant back on the pillows. The L on his keyring made sense now. Of course, it should be an E, but James had always done that sort of thing differently. L-E—she spelt it out to herself as she lay there. She was relieved when James made a move to go. 'I'd better get going. I'm supposed to be getting a haircut at twelve.'

'Of course.' She gave a bright smile. 'Thanks for coming to see me, and for explaining things yesterday—I feel so much better.'

'Good.'

'I'll see you tomorrow then.' He gave a brief frown. He shouldn't have said he'd come and visit her tomorrow. That wasn't a habit he should be forming.

'Of course.' He gave her a smile and there was an awkward moment, when again he chose not to give her a kiss on the cheek. The ease with which he'd pulled her into his arms yesterday was starting to worry him. 'I'll see you tomorrow.'

As he walked back down to the department James's phone buzzed and he stared at the screen, but chose not to answer.

Ellie.

He'd deliberately said her name to Lorna. At the first opportunity he had let Lorna know about Ellie. Because he'd had to, because he'd needed to, because it was right to.

Only he wasn't doing it just to be loyal to his girlfriend.

It was called self-preservation.

CHAPTER SEVEN

'IT'S BRILLIANT GOING out with a doctor!' Ellie laughed as they drove away from what had surely been the most boring wedding reception in the universe. 'You have a permanent excuse to get away early!'

'Good, isn't it?' James smiled.

'So what will we do?'

James wasn't smiling now. Instead he flashed on his indicator and needlessly changed lanes. 'I've got to pop in to a work thing.'

'I could come with you and then we can go back to mine.'

'I've got a lot on tomorrow.'

'You have a day off tomorrow.' He could hear the strained note to her voice and knew that it was merited—they hadn't seen each other all week. He also knew what was coming next—it had been a bone of contention since they'd first started going out. 'Why don't you ever take me to work things, James?'

'You know I like to keep things separate. I told you that from the start.'

'More than a year ago,' Ellie pointed out. 'I think it's a bit much you have to drop me off home to go for one drink with them.'

'Fine,' James said. 'Come!' That took the wind out of Ellie's sails, given that he'd never taken anyone along to a work thing, well, not since Lorna. As they walked through the noisy bar, the emergency team were the noisiest of the lot. They whooped with delight that James had come. Mick was delighted with the gift James had bought him, over and above the collective present. It was a pen James had had engraved, thanking Mick for all his work over the years. But there were a few put-out faces amongst the women and more than a smudge of a frown on May's brow when James first walked in with Ellie.

Still it was one drink and one drink only. Afterwards they headed back to Ellie's and, pulling up outside, he felt like the biggest bastard in the world when he didn't switch off the engine.

'I'm really tired, Ellie,' he said, when she asked why he wasn't coming in.

'I do have a bed!' She tried to make a joke but he heard it wobble midway, heard her tears, because he couldn't bear to see them. 'Don't do this, James.'

And about here he should have said, 'Do what?' Or, 'I'm just tired.' He should have put her mind at rest, except he couldn't, because he was doing what she was begging him not to.

'Look, I just need some space.'

'No,' she said firmly. 'No, you don't. You need to come in with me so we can talk, James.'

'No.' He shook his head, because talking was the last thing he needed. How could he talk when he didn't know what to say, how could he talk when he didn't even know how he felt?

'Ellie, you're a great girl…'

She slapped his cheek and he took it, because she *was* a great girl and it had been, if not great then as close to it as he'd ever got in years, close enough to believe this might, possibly, just about be the one.

'Why?' she demanded. 'Why would you throw it all away?'

'It's not you…'

'No, it's bloody Lorna.'

'It isn't Lorna,' James attempted. 'That's long since over. She's seeing someone.'

'It *is* Lorna!' Ellie said, wrenching open the car door. 'After all she did, after the way she treated you, how could you—?'

'I just need to get my head around things,' James said.

'And you can't do that with me.'

He looked at her then and wished it could be different, but he was honest to a fault—would never consider being unfaithful. Although he and Lorna were hardly going to tumble into bed, although he had absolutely no intention of getting involved with Lorna again, she *was* in his head, which meant he needed to sort that out. He couldn't do that to Ellie. *Wouldn't* do that to Ellie.

'No, Ellie, I can't do it with you. I'm sorry.'

'So you should be.'

She slammed out of the car and up her drive and James wanted to go after her, to tell her just how sorry he was again, except that wouldn't be fair on her.

As he drove off, he was angry—with Lorna.

For coming back into his life just when it was sorted. For messing with his head *again.*

He was driving past the hospital, thought of her up there in bed in those neon pyjamas, and not for a minute did he want their marriage back. It had been hell. In hindsight, Lorna had been right to walk out, to end it without excuse or argument.

And yet, letting himself into his smart London townhouse, he didn't notice Ellie's earrings on the bench or her jacket hanging up in the hall. Instead he went to the cupboard in his bedroom and took down the box he'd always meant to throw out, but never had, and sat on the bed staring at the wedding photos.

She looked so beautiful staring up at him, her amber eyes shining with love. He could remember how he'd felt staring down at her—a mixture of pride and hope laced with certainty. Sure, in that moment that they would make it, that as rushed and as forced on them as this marriage had been, somehow they would be fine. And yet…

They hadn't even seen out the year.

CHAPTER EIGHT

THE TROUBLE WITH being a patient in a teaching
hospital was the teaching!

Oh, it was wonderful to have such excellent
care, and as a doctor herself Lorna had stood
plenty of times at a bedside and listened
intently as the poor patient's innards were discussed, prodded and poked. She too had always
given an apologetic smile to the patient, but it
was hell to be on the receiving end.

Monday morning's ward round seemed to go
on for ever. Her warming, the extensive resuscitation were all discussed at length. The
trauma consultant, Mr Braun, explained how
her seat-belt injury and fractured ribs had been
exacerbated by the cardiac massage and Lorna

could understand now why she was so bruised and sore. The black hole where her brain had been was filling again, her independence returning. When a clumsy student prodded her abdomen, an intensely private Lorna wanted to weep. Then her scars were discussed.

'Ruptured ectopic pregnancy.' The student had done his homework well and read her notes.

'What did they find when they operated?'

'Adhesions from her appendectomy.'

'What other gynaecological problems does Dr McClelland suffer from?'

'Er, endometriosis.'

'Which is relevant to her treatment because?'

She felt sorry for the student, more sorry for herself, but, still, she felt sorry for him as his brain frantically tried to scramble as to how an ectopic pregnancy ten years ago and endometriosis now might be relevant to the injuries she had sustained in the accident.

'Dr McClelland is scheduled to have a hysterectomy early in the new year,' the consultant pushed. 'Why would a thirty-two-year-old woman with no children consider such a radical procedure?'

'For the pain?' the student answered, and let out a relieved breath when Mr Braun nodded. A long discussion ensued as to how hard it had been to get her pain under control when she'd first come out of ICU. She was on particularly strong pain killers now because her tolerance was high as a result of the strong painkillers she had to take to get through her normal life.

'Thank you.' The student gave the familiar apologetic smile as the team drifted out of the room and Lorna gave a rather wobbly one back. She tried not to feel like a thirty-two-year-old childless woman who was electing for a radical procedure. She tried not to think that though on paper she was childless, there had once been a baby, a little heartbeat on the screen, that had meant the world to her—had meant the world to James too.

She could remember the excitement of going

for her antenatal appointment. Newly married, she had also been new to London, having transferred her studies. She had just squeezed onto the full list of the obstetrician at the new teaching hospital, where James had been working and she studying. Pregnancy had suited her. For the first time in her life she'd had if not cleavage then definitely a bust, and her hair had been the shiniest it had ever been. It had even made the morning, noon and night sickness bearable, and there had been this sense of freedom too—away from her parents, married to James, life had seemed pretty much perfect.

Until the registrar had examined her.

Lorna knew she'd been concerned. One minute they had been chatting away about how Lorna was settling into her new medical school, how she would combine finishing off her studies with a new baby, and then as the registrar had probed her stomach, a long silence had fallen.

'I'll just get Mr Arnold in to have a feel.'

Lorna lay there, trying not to panic, trying to

tell herself that everything was okay, only she knew that it wasn't. Still, there would be no quick answer. Mr Arnold was in Theatre and the previously chatty registrar was now rather more aloof, filling in forms at her large desk and ringing the ultrasound department.

'We'll take some blood and then I want you to go down and have an ultrasound.'

'Is there something wrong?'

'Your uterus isn't the size I'd expect.' She gave a poor attempt at a reassuring smile. 'Let's just get the ultrasound.'

Lorna rang James at that point. She was sitting in the corridor, drinking a litre of water as instructed to push up her uterus when he arrived. She could tell he was worried and trying not to show it. He asked her a few times what exactly the registrar had said and was a touch on edge at her lack of answers.

'I know I'm pregnant.' She was desperate to go to the loo now, and angry with the doctor for putting them through all this, because she *knew* that she was. Morning sickness was a good sign of hormone levels according to her textbook and her breasts had almost doubled in size this week alone. 'I was sick this morning,' Lorna said defiantly. She stood when the radiologist called her name.

Kind, polite but business like she asked Lorna to lie down and tucked paper sheets into the top of her panties, poured warm gel over her abdomen. James squeezed Lorna's hand a fraction tighter as the probe moved over and over her stomach. Then there it was, a moment of relief as she heard the sound of her baby, its heart galloping away, except James wasn't smiling and neither was the radiologist.

'If you'll just wait there for a moment.' The radiologist had climbed down from her stool and headed out of the darkened room, leaving the still image of their baby on the screen. Lorna couldn't work out the problem. Oh, she wasn't an expert on scans but there it was, a head, two arms, two legs. They'd only been in for two minutes, for goodness' sake. No measurements had been taken, there was a healthy-sounding heartbeat. What could suddenly be so wrong?

'What is it, James?'

'I'm not sure.'

'James, please…' She knew he was lying, could see his tense jaw, could feel his hand gripping tightly as he tried not to look at her. 'Please just tell me. I know something is wrong.'

'I'm not sure, okay, but…' He paused for a moment before continuing, 'Lorna, I'm really not sure, but I think the baby might not be in the right position.'

The door opened then, admitting not just the radiologist but her obstetrician and the registrar too. Lorna was too shocked to say anything. She lay there, willing her baby well. Maybe the placenta was low and she'd be stuck for weeks on bed rest, maybe…

'Lorna.' It was the first time she'd met Mr Arnold, her obstetrician, and he introduced himself and then shook James's hand before taking over the ultrasound. His face was a picture of intense concentration as again the probe was run over her lower abdomen.

'I'm sorry to have to tell you this, but your pregnancy is ectopic.'

'No.' She refused to accept it.

'Your uterus is empty, Lorna. The foetus has developed in a Fallopian tube.'

'No.' She hated it that suddenly they were calling it a foetus when just a few minutes ago it had been her baby.

'The foetus isn't viable.'

'The baby,' Lorna interrupted.

She completely refused to accept it, refused to listen when they told her that at any moment the tube might rupture, that there was no choice but to have the foetus removed. It was James who had to deal with it all. It was James who held her hand when they gently examined her and then checked their findings with ultrasound again. The terminology had changed—her baby wasn't a baby any more, rather a foetus, but she could still see it moving and wriggling on the screen, still hear the whoosh, whoosh, whoosh of its little heartbeat.

'Could you turn off the sound?' It was the first time in her life that she had shouted and, Lorna realised, it worked. The room stilled for a moment, the sound of her baby's heart filling the tense air, then the technician flicked a switch and as easily as that the sound of her baby's heartbeat was obliterated.

The obstetrician left then, leaving his registrar to complete the necessary paperwork. Only Lorna didn't want to go directly to Theatre, didn't want to face the inevitable result.

'I feel fine.'

'You have to go to Theatre.' She could see the tears in James's green eyes as he forced her to see sense. 'If it ruptures, and it will rupture,' James said clearly, 'I don't want to lose you both.'

'Can we just go home?' Even as she said it, she knew how insane it sounded, and moved swiftly to clarify what she meant. 'I just need a night to get my head around it.'

'Lorna.' The registrar was nicer than her boss. Strict but kind, she spelt out the facts, held Lorna's hand and took her through it step by step—only despite the registrar's calm demeanour there was a flurry of activity going on in the room. An IV had been inserted into Lorna's arm, blood had been taken for a cross-match and a bag of saline was now hanging and dripping into her veins, to keep the line open, the registrar said, *just in case.*

Lorna knew what those words meant—on her emergency rotation she'd seen a woman rushed to Theatre, pale and exsanguinated. Her undiagnosed ectopic pregnancy had ruptured. At any moment, Lorna was being told, this could happen to her. *Would* happen to her, the registrar said gently but firmly, reiterating that from everything they could see on the ultrasound, rupture was imminent.

A consent form was there in front of her.

Just that morning she and James had been good-naturedly arguing about whether to find out the sex. Lorna wanted to know so she could make lots of lists and choose names and colours. James preferred to wait, to enjoy the surprise of whatever they were given.

Now they were asking Lorna to sign a death warrant.

'We'll try and preserve the tube,' the registrar explained again, 'but till we get in and have a look…'

'No.' Lorna said it again in the hope someone would listen. She could see James was losing his patience, his jaw tense. He got up to pace the room as a nurse came in and slipped off Lorna's clothes and taped over her ring even though she was refusing the procedure.

'We'll just take off your nail varnish.' Lorna could smell the acetone and it made her gag. She wished James would do something—he was a doctor, for crying out loud.

'Even the examination we just performed

could have exacerbated things,' the registrar explained. 'It's low in your Fallopian tube and it's too large for drug treatment. If we let you go home and it ruptures, James is right, we could lose you both.'

'There's nothing you can do?' Lorna begged. 'I saw a show once, this woman in India.'

'Lorna.' James interrupted her pleadings. 'The pregnancy can't continue.'

There was no way out—her ectopic pregnancy was at imminent risk of rupture. The pregnancy could not continue and there wasn't a single thing Lorna could do to change the facts.

She could still remember signing the consent form—laparoscopy for ectopic pregnancy, removal of POC and salpingectomy.

'POC?'

If it had been any day before this one, Lorna would have soon worked it out, except she felt as if her brain had been left on ice and was drifting into winter.

'Product of conception,' the registrar translated. 'And we'll do everything we can to preserve the Fallopian tube, but if we have to, we need your permission to perform a salpingectomy, which is the removal of the tube.'

Lorna started to vomit then, though not as she had that morning. Giddy nausea swept over her and she could see James's look of alarm as the registrar turned up the drip and paged her boss.

'Just sign the form, Lorna.'

Why couldn't he sign it? She could remember looking at him and thinking it. If it was so bloody easy, why couldn't it be him that signed? Except nothing about this was easy, so instead Lorna took the offered pen and signed the form. Then, dizzy, she lay back as she was rushed straight to Theatre.

'Hey!' He was standing at the door and though he gave her a smile, Lorna could tell it was a guarded one. He'd brought two vast take-away cups of coffee and what she assumed was her phone charger in a plastic bag. 'Sorry I didn't get in yesterday.'

'That's fine.' Lorna smiled. 'I was hardly going anywhere.'

He handed her the package and Lorna opened it, wincing as she turned to her bedside table to get her phone. James did it for her, plugging in the charger and making small talk, but awkwardly.

'Thanks for the coffee.' Lorna took a grateful sip. 'I'm starting to look forward to it, the hospital stuff is disgusting.'

'Tell me about it!' He sat down and she was glad that he did. Clearly she was getting better because she was at times bored. As a courtesy probably, because she was a doctor, she had her own little side room, but being so far from home, there were no visitors to look forward to and there was way too much time to think. Still, Lorna consoled herself, at least now she had her phone.

'I saw the mob in the corridor. Have they got to you yet?'

'Yes, they just finished. I'm doing very well apparently. I might even get home on Wednesday.'

'That's good.'

It wasn't, actually. For Lorna it was daunting.

'So will you go to your friend's?'

'I don't think so. She's away for another week and returning to find me in this state might be stretching the boundaries of friendship.'

'Will you go to your parents', then?'

Lorna hesitated before answering. 'I guess I'll have to. I don't know…' Just the thought of sitting in the car for the six-hour drive with her ribcage like this was bad enough, but with her father driving… Lorna closed her eyes at the horror of moving back there.

'You don't seem too pleased at the prospect. Are you not getting on?'

'We haven't got on for years, James.'

'They were desperately worried about you.'

'I'm their daughter,' Lorna said. 'They love me, of course they were worried when I was injured. They weren't at all pleased that I was thinking of moving back to London. This is proof to them that I shouldn't come.'

Her phone bleeped then, more than a week's worth of calls and texts all there, worried friends and family no doubt. She scrolled through them quickly, would get back to them later. It was actually the interview callbacks she really needed to hear about.

'Do you want me to go?' James offered, but she shook her head, rolling her eyes as she played back her messages, her pale cheeks tinging pink as four times, though nicely, though regretfully, she found out she'd been rejected.

'Well, now I really do wish I'd just stayed home that day!' She attempted a bright smile, but it faltered. 'I don't have enough experience…'

'You're a great doctor.'

'You never knew me as a doctor,' Lorna pointed out, 'but, yes, I am. I'm just not the one they want for the job.' She gave a small shrug, but it hurt to do so and she grimaced, not at the job loss but at the pain.

'Do you need something for pain?' James checked.

'I had something an hour ago.'

'Well, it isn't working. They can be mean with painkillers.' He stood up and picked up her chart, a doctor through and through. It didn't enter his head that it might be intrusive. 'You need to be doing some deep breathing and coughing if you don't want to get a chest infection and two paracetamol aren't...' His voice trailed off. He even blinked a couple of times when he saw just how strong the painkillers were that she was on.

'I'm on plenty.' Lorna tried to make light of it. 'It just hurts, that's all. Apart from getting someone to knock me out, I'm just going to have to put up with it.' She could see his worried features as he sat down. 'Mr Braun did the rounds this morning and he explained how long the cardiac massage went on for. Add that to fractured ribs and a seat-belt injury, well, I'm just going to have to put up with it for a while.'

'That bruise.' James pointed to his own chest,

but they both knew he meant hers. 'How far does it go?'

'Down to my stomach, under my arms. It really is quite spectacular!' It was, black and purple now, smudged with dirty yellow around the edges. In Emergency she'd been lily white with just a few shiny new blue bruises, with her hypothermia there had been no real sign of the extensive bruising that would follow.

'You poor thing.' James said simply, and it was said in such a way that it was more a fact he delivered, a statement that touched somewhere inside, made her feel like someone understood, because bruising and rib fractures didn't really describe the battering her body had taken. 'Lorna,' James said, 'you can't go home on Wednesday.'

'I know,' she answered, because since Mr. Braun had said that an hour or so ago, her mind had been going like a table-tennis ball, pinging back and forward with possibilities. As well as dealing with the pain, as well as remembering her baby, as well as seeing James, even if she looked as if she was just lying back on the pillow, she was multitasking. 'I've been thinking of going to a hotel for a few days.'

'A hotel?'

'That's what they do now for some women when they've had a baby—rather than take up a hospital bed, they send them—'

'Lorna!'

'It's a good idea! Meals sent up, fresh towels, the bed made and then when I'm feeling up to the journey…well, I'll think about that then.'

'You'll stay with me.' It was as simple and as complicated as that.

'How?' Lorna asked. A single word but there were so many questions behind it. 'I just need to rest, James.'

'You can do that at my place.'

'How?' she asked again, because quite simply she wasn't up to raking over the past, or catching up to the present. She wasn't sure that moving in with her ex, even if it was just for a few days, was a good idea.

'Look—we're adults.' James clearly had the same set of questions. 'We were over a long time ago, we've both moved on, but we *were* married and, yes, I do care. I'm sure if the roles were reversed, you'd do the same for me?' She heard the question and she nodded.

'Of course I would.'

'So it's simple. I'll be at work most of the time and I'm not going to be demanding answers about the past or anything like that. Anyway, you've got your guy in Africa.'

'Africa?'

'Kenya,' James said, and Lorna started laughing.

'Did my Dad tell you that?'

'Oh, yes.' James grinned. 'When he told me not to come and see you!'

'He's unbelievable!' Lorna snarled. 'I haven't seen Matthew in two years! You know I feel sorry for unconscious people—it's bad enough being half-dead, let alone having people talking for you who haven't got a clue what you want.'

James laughed, glimpsed for the first time the old Lorna McClelland, her fiery little ways, her strange thought processes that had once made him smile. Lorna would have laughed again, too. Actually she started to, but it hurt too much so she gave up.

'So that's settled, then.' James stood up. 'I'll take the morning off on Wednesday and take you home and get you settled.' He frowned down at her. 'Actually, I'll take the day off.'

'You don't have to.'

'Just the first day, till you're settled.'

'Thank you.' Lorna said.

'Your father's not going to be too pleased.' He half expected her to come up with some convoluted way to lie to her father, just as she had in the past, but instead she lay back on the pillow and gave the small shrug her bruised chest would allow.

'Oh, well.'

* * *

Lorna woke late afternoon, confused.

She was in a swirling place and her frantic eyes searched for James.

'It's okay, Lorna.' A nameless voice was taking her blood pressure. 'You're in hospital.'

Only she wasn't soothed, she was stuck somewhere between the past and the present, lying in a hospital bed and trying to work out what had happened.

She'd loathed waking without James after her surgery, wanted him to be the one to tell her what had happened to their baby, but he'd bccn ringing her parents and updating them when the registrar had come round.

She was a 'lucky girl', apparently. The Fallopian tube had ruptured about five minutes before they had gone in.

"It's no wonder you're sore,' the registrar had said, upping her pain control and telling her how difficult the procedure had been. The gluey cobweb of adhesions from her appendectomy had enclosed the Fallopian tube. It had been the first glimpse of the problems she had, but at the time it had been easier to ignore them, far easier not to think or ask about the future.

'Hey.' He sat down by her bed and took her hand. 'You're awake! I was just ringing your parents.'

'How were they?'

'Concerned,' James said, kissing her forehead. 'But I've told them you're okay… I saw the reg in the corridor. Has she been in?'

'Just.'

'What did she say?'

'Lorna?' The nurse was fiddling with her IV, dragging her back to the present and asking if she had any pain, to which Lorna nodded.

'Could you turn down the infusion?' she asked, to the nurse's confusion, but Lorna was too tired to explain.

The pain of the present she could deal with, it was the past and the future she didn't want to drift into.

* * *

'Pauline.' James ran a slightly exasperated hand through his hair as he eyed his home through Lorna's eyes. 'We're getting a guest.'

That he was even considering discussing with his daily that they hire a cleaner was less a reflection on Lorna's neatness and more a reflection on Pauline's lack of it.

He could never consider getting rid of Pauline.

It would be like asking your mother to leave.

Your messy, disorganised, borderline alcoholic mother, perhaps, but at least she knew how he liked his toast. At least she knew that when a telephone marketer rang at 10 a.m. when he was on nights, 'Professor Morrell' was not to be disturbed.

Girlfriends had come and gone, pointing out that Pauline did nothing bar empty the dishwasher, shuffle the mess, watch pay TV and make inroads into his whisky—all true. Only not once in the five years she had been with him had James had to think about buying toothpaste, or even a toothbrush, had to iron his shirt, or wonder if there was anything to eat.

Pauline took care of that.

Her chatter drove him crazy—the Irish loved to tell a tale and Pauline certainly could—but, then, the time her knee had played up, to his surprise, he'd missed her moaning.

Whatever dinner she made at home—and her cooking was fabulous—was divided and plated for James and placed in his fridge. If she treated herself and her husband to a chocolate bar, she treated James too. It would be there waiting for him on the kitchen bench when he came home at two a.m., and after a Saturday night in Emergency, being insulted or dealing with a suicide, well, that chocolate bar was welcome, but more the sentiment behind it— especially when it was accompanied by one of her notes. 'An Englishman walked into a bar...' Somehow, Pauline made James feel as if he had come home, and if she hired a movie and liked it, well, it was there waiting, too, on those nights he couldn't wind down from work and sleep.

A couple of years ago Pauline had taken a month off to go on a cruise with her husband, and James had fast realised that whatever she didn't do, she made up for with what she did do. She was talking about going on another cruise next year and James was already not looking forward to it.

'What sort of guest?' Pauline asked, wiping down the bench and working out her excuses, because if his mother was coming again, then her knee was suddenly hurting.

'Her name's Lorna.' The awkwardness in his voice made her look up, her dishcloth pausing in midswipe as James elaborated. 'My ex-wife.'

She'd known something was up. Her best friend, May, had been dropping hints like a semaphore signaller for well over a week now, but never in her wildest dreams would Pauline have guessed there had once been a Mrs Morrell.

'Your ex-wife, you say?' Pauline stopped

cleaning the bench and started loading bread into the toaster—pulling ham and cheese out of the fridge and taking a long time to find the jar of capers. 'I never knew you'd been married.' She said to a dozen eggs. She came out of the fridge with a smile on her face. 'Well, fancy that!'

'It was ages ago,' James said, flicking open the paper and pretending to read it. 'She's been in a car accident and isn't well enough yet to travel home.'

'And where's home?'

'Scotland.' James answered. 'Fife.'

'She's a Fifer.'

'No,' James said tartly, 'she's from Glasgow, but now she's in Fife. She'll only be here for a few days, but she'll need to stay in my room.'

'Your room?'

James looked up from the horoscope he was reading. 'She's sick—I've got an en suite. Can you freshen up the place and make me up a bed in the spare room? Lorna's a bit…'

'A bit what?' Pauline pushed.

'Fussy.' James said, then added. 'Your phone's bleeping.'

It was too!

A message from May.

Half day 2morrow—coffee in morning?

Can't. Pauline texted back. *Have to work—guest arriving.*

Need a hand?

Pauline thought of James's shower that she hadn't visited in a while, the sheets that needed washing and changing, the ex-wife who was about to descend, and as James bit into his toasted sandwich, Pauline hit the send button.

Please.

May and Pauline had been friends for years. Even though they had grown up near each other, they had only met in London when Pauline had been an orderly on a gynaecology ward and May had been a staff nurse. They had struck up an instant friendship that had easily grown, given how well their husbands got on too.

It had only dawned on Pauline in mid-interview, when James had been telling her about his rather erratic hours, that he was *the* 'lovely Dr James' that May sometimes mentioned. Some sixth sense had told her to keep quiet, that if her prospective boss knew that her best friend happened to work alongside him, then she wouldn't get the job.

And she wanted it.

An ex-wife was very different from a new girlfriend.

With as much gusto as if his mother *were* coming, she changed sheets, sorted out the linen cupboard, wiped down the cutlery drawer and cleaned the fridge. In fact, she was kneeling on a rolled-up piece of towel, trying to coax a bit of jelly from last Christmas to melt, when May arrived, bunches of flowers in hand.

'If James comes home suddenly…' Pauline fretted, but May shook her head.

'The place is steaming—he won't be home for hours yet. Let's get to work.'

'We'll be sailing on the seven seas this time next year,' May reminded her as she sprayed the shower and Pauline took down the screen to soak it. 'Just think about that.'

CHAPTER NINE

PATIENTS often didn't realise just how ill they were when they're in hospital.

It's only when they went back into the real world and met the million and one things that made it real that they suddenly realised how poorly or sore they really were. And for Lorna the realisation came as she stood up in the wheelchair at the collection point and tried to lower herself into James's rather low sports car. Even putting on her seat belt herself was impossible. She couldn't twist to get it and neither could she easily twist to clip it—two simple manoeuvres that she'd never really given a thought to until now.

'I'll do it.'

He leant carefully over her and it was, for

Lorna, their first contact, his big shoulders so close, his hair in her face. He smelt different but the same, so big and strong and efficient and gentle.

'Ouch!' Tears stung her eyes and she felt like the biggest baby in the world, but as he leant back and released the seat belt the pressure was unbearable.

'God, Lorna, I'm sorry.' He pulled at the belt and held it loose, unclipped it again and looked at her with concerned eyes. 'Just wait there.'

He darted into Emergency and came back with a pillow, which she held on her chest as he again went through the rigmarole of clipping her in.

And that was before she'd even got out of the hospital. Everything on the five-minute journey to his home was daunting, the winter sun too bright, the sound of a siren as fire engines raced towards them on the other side of the road made her sweat. Her memory of the accident had returned now. Not that she'd told anyone, but she could remember well the loss of control, the screech of the tyres, the slam of metal as she'd hit a tree. Now even going at twenty miles an hour in the busy London traffic felt way too fast.

'Nearly there.' James glanced over but she wished he wouldn't. She wanted him to keep his eyes on the road.

He had a lovely town house in Islington and he held her arm as slowly she climbed the steps, utterly exhausted by the time she got inside.

'It's lovely!' Lorna blinked at the gleaming furniture, the flowers in the vases. It was nothing like she was used to from James!

'I've got a surprise for you!' He waited till she'd lowered herself onto the chair.

'A surprise?'

He held up a bag and then opened it, pulled out pyjamas and dressing gown in soft pinks and greens, slippers, leggings and fluffy socks and lots of *nice* things.

'You shouldn't have.'

'I didn't.' James said. 'It's from May. The pyjamas are new, but the dressing gown and other things are her daughter's. She's off travelling for a year.'

'That's so kind of her.'

'She's a lovely woman,' James said, 'thoughtful, you know. Anyway—' his face was deadpan as he spoke, just the same way it used to be when he joked with her '—I couldn't have let you move in here wearing those. They truly are the most disgusting pyjamas I've ever seen and they keep getting worse.'

'It was a pack of three,' Lorna said glumly. 'Orange, pink and baby pooh green. I like to think my mother just has no taste, but I'm sure the fact James Morrell was there sent her searching the shops for the ugliest sleepwear in history, to stop him from fancying me.'

'Well, good for Betty.' James grinned. 'Because it worked!'

'I'll put them on when Ellie comes round.' Lorna carried on the joke. 'Just in case she's worried that your ex is here!'

He didn't say anything—he certainly wasn't

going to tell her they'd broken up. That *would* have her worried, would stop the easygoing banter that was starting to come. Lorna knew his rules, knew he would never so much as look at another woman while he was already with one. There was just no need to confuse things. When Lorna admitted she was tired, he helped her up the stairs and took her into the master bedroom. He had upped Pauline's hours and insisted the room have the biggest spring clean of its life since Monday.

'I can't take your room.'

'It's got its own toilet and shower,' James said, 'and a nice view of the street so you don't get too bored!'

'Way better than the hospital generator,' Lorna agreed.

'Do you want a shower?'

'No thanks.' She shook her head. 'I just want to sleep.'

'Go for it, then.' He pulled the curtains and the room was bathed in lovely darkness, so dark he had to turn on the side-light. 'I bought decent curtains, this room gets the sun and it's hell trying to get to sleep in a bright room after working all night.' Suddenly it was awkward, so he headed for the door. 'Have a nice rest.'

She did, slid into bed and slept for a solid four hours, only waking again because she started coughing and the painkillers had worn off. She was relieved that James had stayed home for her first day here. She heard his footsteps on the stairs, a knock on the door. He must have been dozing himself, because his face had that lovely sort of crumpled look to it, and his hair was sticking up at the side.

'Here,' he said, giving her a drink of water and her lunchtime medicines. 'I'll get you some lunch.'

'I'm not hungry.'

'I wasn't asking if you were. I'm making lunch and you'll eat it whether you want it or not.'

'You have to be nice to me, remember.' Lorna smiled. 'Because I'm sick.'

Oh, and he had to bite his tongue. He was about to remind her that he'd always been nice to her, sick or not, that he'd always tried to do the right thing by her.

Only he'd also promised her that he wouldn't go over the past.

CHAPTER TEN

'I NEED to listen to your chest.'

James loved his job, but at times the system frustrated him. Lorna had dozed after lunch and slept most of the evening, eating some of the chicken soup he'd brought for her and drinking a glass of water as per his instructions. She promptly went back to sleep, only to wake after midnight, coughing and crying and coughing some more. This patient should not have been sent home, aside from the fact that her home was a six-hour drive away, it was too soon for a layperson to be expected to look after her. Worse, James thought as he leant her forward and listened to her chest, was the idea of her lying in a hotel room, coughing and in pain, with no one to look after her. No, this patient should be in a hospital bed, James said to himself as, embarrassed for her, he helped Lorna with her buttons and listened to the front of her chest.

The bruising *was* appalling. He had been slightly taken aback by the strength of her analgesics, but, hey, seeing the bruising, he accepted it now.

No wonder she'd sobbed when he'd put on the seat belt. Lorna was the toughest woman he knew, and for just a flash, a little flash, he remembered that first night home after her operation. Lorna had been in pain, but had lain quietly beside him and not once acknowledged it. How he'd wished that she had.

'A few creps…' He pulled off his stethoscope. He'd checked her temp and it was on the high side of normal, but James was sure it had recently been otherwise. Despite her urgent coughing, regular deep breathing was proving difficult, which meant, given the noise he had heard on her chest, that a chest infection was brewing.

'You ought to be re-admitted.' He saw her anguished look. 'Okay, we'll start you on some antibiotics, but if things don't turn around quickly, you'll have to go back for a chest X-ray. You need to do more deep breathing and coughing.'

'I can't *stop* coughing!'

James headed over to work. It was a trip he was used to making in the middle of the night and he smiled when he saw May.

'Did we call you in?' May asked.

'Nope. I'm here for myself, well, Lorna actually. She's recuperating at my place for a few days before she goes back to Scotland.' He chatted as he wrote out a script and gave it to May. The emergency department carried a supply of drugs that could be dispensed at night, and May found a bottle of antibiotics while James took a vial and a needle and syringe.

'I'll give her an IM shot and then hopefully

she'll be okay on oral. How long are you on nights for?'

'A couple of weeks. All the senior staff are having to pitch in,' May tutted. 'I know it's not the time or place, but we are so short of medical staff, there's too much falling on the nurses.'

'We're interviewing,' James said. 'There are more ads in the papers this week. That's all we can do at the moment.'

'Well, tell Lorna to hurry up and get well.'

'I'm hardly going to work with my ex-wife, May.' He grinned as she walked with him through the department.

'Well, she's staying with you, so you clearly get on and Ellie can't mind. She's a nice girl, Ellie.'

'She is.'

'It was nice to meet her.'

Driving home, there was a certain disquiet in James as he realised for the second time that day he had chosen to let people think Ellie and he were still an item. It was easier, James consoled himself, far, far easier than letting

May get ideas. And as for Lorna…walking back into the house, he still hadn't come up with an answer to that one.

'That *does* hurt!' Funny that Lorna was less embarrassed getting a penicillin shot in the bottom from James than from some strange nurse. He was so matter-of-fact and so…James. The only real discomfort was the needle.

'Yes, but it works,' he said as she settled back on the pillows. 'I stopped at the petrol station and bought you some blackcurrant cordial. You're not drinking enough.' He returned a couple of minutes later with a big glass of her favourite drink when she was ill and made her drink the lot.

'Right.' He sat on the side of the bed. 'I *have* to go to work tomorrow. I don't want to. In fact, I don't think you should be on your own.'

'I'll be fine.'

'Listen,' James interrupted, not up to small talk at two a.m. 'We're short on doctors, the place is struggling, so I *have* to be there, *but* I'm five minutes away. If we get a lull I'll come home. Also I'll ask my cleaning lady to stay a couple of hours extra.' He grinned at her wide-eyed look. 'Do you think the house looks like this by itself? Actually, even with Pauline, it doesn't normally look this good. She's really gone to town for you coming. Usually it's a bit chaotic, she's not exactly obsessively tidy, but she is kind and sort of...' He tried to think of the word. 'Sort of a mum.'

'Not my sort of mum, I hope!' Lorna said. 'That's the last thing I need.' Which made her smile, which made him laugh, which made her laugh too, which of course made her cough.

'Get some sleep,' James said once her coughing fit was over. 'I'll put my head in in the morning, but I won't wake you.'

'Thank you,' Lorna said. Then she said it again, but with different emphasis, so grateful he was there, that he had stepped in and that it was James looking after her during this horrible time. 'Thank you.'

'You're more than welcome.'

'And I am sorry,' Lorna added, 'for all the trouble.'

'These things are sent to try us!' James said in a Scottish accent, mimicking her father as he had never been able to before, and when she laughed he was relieved that she did.

Oh, she was trouble all right. Despite her prim little ways and her assurances that she would be gone in just a few days, James knew that as he stretched out in his rather basic spare room a whole pile of trouble had just landed in his life and upended it.

CHAPTER ELEVEN

IT WAS actually easy having Lorna when she was clearly ill. Pain, medicine, soup and coughs, all those James could deal with. She was safely holed up in his bedroom after all. Apart from a couple of daily visits and the odd chat on the sofa, it was like having a sick relative staying to recuperate, or at least that was how James coped with it.

If he wasn't already at the hospital, he rose at six-thirty, fell out of bed, peeked into her room to check she was asleep and comfortable then went for a quick run before heading for work. Pauline was around for the most part, and generally by the time he came home Lorna was either in bed or just about to go up. So far it had worked and kept a nice firm wedge between them. In the last few days she was sometimes up by the time he returned from his run, his cup of tea already made for him, and they shared a quick chat about the weather before he went to work. Oh, she was more than a patient for sure—he usually didn't scoop them off the trolleys and bring them home after all, but with the complication of a chest infection, the couple of days turned into more and it wasn't until the second week came around that Lorna turned *the* corner. She was off her antibiotics, her bruising fading, her colour and humour returning, and suddenly she didn't need a doctor any more—which was all James knew how to be around her.

All James felt *safe* being around her.

'Morning.' Returning from his run, there was tea and toast this time and Lorna looking like Lorna always had in the morning. She was wearing mint-green pyjamas that were way too big, but, then, everything always was on her, and a pair of his socks. Her long auburn hair was tied in a loose knot and hung on one side of her chest. Her glasses were perched on her nose and the paper was spread out on the table. It was at that precise second that James realised that in every woman who had uttered the 'Morning' word to him, he had been hoping for this, that her smile or her chatter would eventually grow to feel like *this*.

A mixture of peace and excitement, of home and familiarity and just plain old desire— because he wanted Lorna so badly. He wanted to take off her glasses and take her up to bed, or he wanted to untie her hair and make love to her, right there in the kitchen, or pull her onto his lap and kiss that familiar face.

But instead he sat down and ate his toast.

'What are you doing today?'

'I've got to ring up the car insurance and Pauline's going to bring me some clothes.'

'She's twice the size of you.' James laughed.

'But we have the same size feet.' Lorna grinned.

'I can't believe your parents haven't sent your clothes.'

'I can!' Lorna rolled her eyes and then carried on reading the paper.

'I take it they're not too pleased at you staying here.' James couldn't help himself. 'What did they say?'

'Not much.' Lorna shrugged. 'They're just not talking to me again.'

'Again?'

'Again.' Lorna smiled and looked up at him and it was just a glance, or it should have been, except he was looking at her in a different way, a way of old, and Lorna found she couldn't tear her eyes from his.

She could feel the skin on her face burning, yet still she couldn't look away and nothing was said, not a single word was exchanged, but if you could kiss without touching, he was kissing her now. This look, where the other knew what the other was thinking and he wasn't a doctor and she wasn't the patient any more, was what did it.

Desire had entered the building. Loudly Pauline rapped on the door and then let herself in.

'I'm going to ring and find out the train times.' They were both pretending nothing had happened and in reality nothing had, only they both knew different.

'There's no rush.' He attempted a nonchalant shrug, his head a mire of contrary thoughts. He wanted her to stay, but he was desperate for her to leave. Because Lorna McClelland and James Morrell didn't work.

He had the divorce papers upstairs to prove it, James reminded himself as he said goodbye and headed for work.

There was a rush, Lorna reminded herself as she punched two tablets out of the blister pack when he had gone and curled up on the bed, holding her stomach. She willed the pain to pass. It was always worse mid-cycle, even though she was on the Pill, even though she was on the strongest painkillers she could take and still function, all they did was take off the edge and her tablets were fast running out. The supply the hospital had dispensed her was almost finished and the bottle that had been in her bag must be lying on the floor of her wrecked car because despite frantic searching she couldn't find it.

Maybe she should just tell James, Lorna thought, lying there willing the cramping to pass, except she couldn't stand to see the pity in his eyes. He'd known how much she wanted children and he had wanted them too.

Five of them, he had joked on their wedding night, stroking her tummy and telling her that this was just the start.

'I know it was rushed…' She could barely get her head around it, she was married to James, his ring was on her finger, the man she had loved from afar for ages was now the man she would spend the rest of her life with. She'd never been so happy, she just needed to know he felt the same. 'I know my dad was awful, that he forced you—'

'Lorna.' James interrupted her with a deep kiss. 'It's our wedding night—can we please not talk about your father?'

Coming home that evening, he found her, glasses on and frowning in concentration as she bent over in the living room and painted her toenails. It was such a familiar sight, stirred up so many familiar feelings that James was seriously worried.

'Pauline lent it to me!' She beamed at her ten glossy toes all separated with balls of cotton wool and on display on the coffee-table. 'I feel human again!' Lorna added as James took one look and headed for the kitchen.

'Good.'

Her father had never let her wear make-up, and from the age of eleven Lorna had painted her toenails—a little act of rebellion that stayed safely in her slippers or shoes.

'I rang up about trains for Glasgow and I've booked for Sunday morning.'

'Good.' James said again, because he couldn't live like this much longer, couldn't stand remembering. He pulled out a casserole that Pauline must have made, but on second thoughts it may have been Lorna. Only Lorna stood and peeled the vegetables over newspaper then wrapped the peels in a tight little ball and threw it in the bin. 'Did you make the casserole?'

'Pauline did!' Lorna called from the living room, her voice getting closer as she walked into join him. 'I just helped with the vegetables—it was my occupational therapy for the day,' she joked. James wasn't smiling. He served up two dinners and tried not to remember what they'd once had. It was like being back there, back in their tiny little flat with their tiny little kitchen, which she'd kept so neat it had driven him crazy. He'd wanted to haul her into bed, to lie in the little island they'd created and watch TV and read and make love and talk and read and make love, not take down curtains and arrange cupboards.

'Are you not hungry?' She frowned as, instead of herself, it was James who was pushing his dinner around the plate.

'I had a sandwich at work.'

'That didn't used to stop you.' Lorna's voice trailed off, realizing that he was uncomfortable. They struggled through the rest of the meal in a rather strained silence, save a couple of comments about how different the hard London water tasted compared to Scotland's, and that he had to remember to put the rubbish out tonight because Pauline had forgotten.

Not exactly riveting stuff, but it got them through dinner.

'I've got a surprise!' She saved it till after dinner. Lorna had half decided that, given the sudden tension, maybe she should just go to bed, but she was bored with bed and tired of having only Pauline to talk to, and anyway she had missed him all day! When James had loaded the dishwasher he came back to the lounge to find her setting up her favourite board game. 'Look what Pauline brought over for me!'

He laughed and groaned at the same time. 'Look, maybe another time—I really have had a shocking day.'

'Then you need to relax!' Lorna smiled up at him. The board was neatly set up. He'd have looked a right old misery if he refused to play— she'd been so ill after all.

She beat him, of course, guarding the diction- ary and challenging him on every word, and it was fun and it was nice, but it was just too much of a glimpse of all that they'd lost. By the time it was ten, James was only too glad to pounce on her first yawn and tell her it was time for bed.

'I'll put the game away,' he added, because they'd always argued over that. Lorna used to want to leave everything just so, while James had always wanted to head for bed. Another sign of their incompatibility—only it wasn't there tonight.

'Leave it.' Lorna shrugged. 'It will still be there in the morning.'

'You've changed your tune,' James said, and suddenly it felt as if they were back at the dinner table, trying not to compare the past with the present, trying not to remember how it had been once—only, unlike James, Lorna wasn't uncomfortable with it.

'Have you only just noticed?' Lorna smiled and for the first time when she said goodnight she kissed him on the cheek, but as she slipped into bed the smile she'd worn all evening faded.

What the hell was she doing?

She knew what it was called, knew that she *had* been flirting. Not deliberately, of course. James was off limits, *they* were off limits. She knew that, and so did James—she'd heard the relief in his voice when she'd told him that on Sunday she'd be gone.

Yes, Lorna told herself, two more nights and apart from a thank-you card, they'd never have to be in contact again—and they'd both surely be better off for it.

James left early for work the next morning, even by his standards. Usually she was up around seven and they'd have a little chat before he headed off, but she heard the front door close and his car start up and somehow she knew James was avoiding her.

He was.

The two nights they had left seemed to stretch into infinity, her scent was everywhere, so were magazines and nail varnish. Her laughter had crept into his home as she'd crept back into his life and he resisted the intrusion at every turn, but there was no escape. Her name cropped up at work, his colleagues enquiring as to how she was doing. Even knowing she was at home made it harder to focus on his day. Still, it was not for much longer. He'd work late tonight, James told himself, he might even crash in the on-call room and, though he'd promised to take her clothes shopping on Saturday, once that was out of the way, he'd head back into work and see as little of her as possible.

It had been easier when she'd been ill.

Every day there were changes, every day there was progress, and this Friday was no exception. Instead of Lorna's usual quick shower, Pauline ran her a bath and sat on the top of the stairs, calling out ever five minutes or so as Lorna lay in the lovely warm, bubbly water, conditioner soaking in her hair, and pinched James's razor to tackle a few neglected areas.

She must have been feeling seriously better because afterwards, instead of collapsing from exhaustion into bed for her usual afternoon doze, for the first time she had a teeny rummage in his cupboards and realised that James did live alone. Apart from a can of ladies' deodorant and a box of tampons there wasn't much *Elliedence* at all. Not even one lousy hair tie! But there was a hairdryer lurking beneath the sink and it was lovely to sit on a bar stool in the kitchen as Pauline blow-dried her long auburn curls. She insisted Lorna would catch her death otherwise.

'How long have you worked for James?' Lorna asked as Pauline moaned about the stairs and how hard it was cleaning for a bear of man who didn't know where the bin was!

'Since a couple of months after he moved in,' Pauline said. 'It would be more than five years now. He's nice to work for, though we have our moments. Not with James, just his...' Her voice sort of stopped then, halted in mid-sentence, and Lorna could only smile.

'I'm his *ex*-wife, Pauline!'

'Well, like I said, I don't mind James and his mess, though it does drive me to distraction at times, but when some madam who's only been here five minutes starts demanding I do her ironing, or moans that there's some hair in the shower...' Lorna smothered another smile as Pauline continued drying her hair. Pauline was adorable, absolutely, but Lorna could picture

Pauline's face if Lorna had suddenly demanded that she iron for her. 'The latest one's not so bad.'

'Ellie,' Lorna said brightly, just so that Pauline knew that she knew James had a girlfriend.

'Mmm.' Pauline said, which wasn't much of an insight.

'I haven't seen much of Ellie.' Lorna was glad she had her back to Pauline. Her face turned purple as she asked the question that had been irking for a couple of days. 'I hope she isn't put out that I'm here.'

'She's away a lot,' Pauline said, blasting Lorna's head with hot air and tugging it tight with the brush. 'She has some fancy job that means a lot of travel. She wouldn't mind anyway—she knows he'd never cheat. James just isn't like that.'

'No.' Lorna swallowed, because she was right. It wouldn't enter James's head to cheat.

'He's a nice man all round really,' Pauline said, 'well, from what I've seen. I'm sure you've got your tale to tell, but apart from his mess, he's a real sweetheart—good looking, funny—*sexy*.' Pauline added in a loud whisper, which made Lorna laugh. She wasn't laughing a second later. In fact, if she didn't know better she'd have sworn Pauline had just tapped her on the head not too lightly with the hairbrush, but of course she hadn't. Pauline apologised quickly that the brush had slipped. So Lorna just sat there, enjoying the hot air on her scalp and Pauline's idle chatter, even answering when it was merited, but her mind was in another place. James *was* a nice man—the fact she was here today proved it. He was also good looking, funny and sexy too, and one who deserved so much more than she was able to give him.

'That looks better!' Pauline deemed her dry enough to survive and Lorna stepped down from the stool. 'You look almost normal.'

It was a compliment. Today she'd not only had a bath but had graduated from pyjamas to leggings and was wearing one of James's rugby shirts. If he had time at the weekend he'd said that he'd take her shopping so she could buy some clothes for her trip back home.

'So are you going back to stay at your friend's?' Pauline shooed her over to the sofa where Lorna, just a bit drained now, was quite glad to lie down and chat as Pauline flicked the television on and settled in for another hour of a self-help show.

'I leave on Sunday. My friend's looking for a couple of rental properties for me, but I can stay there for now till something comes up.'

'What about your parents?' Pauline asked. 'Why don't you stay with them till you're well?'

'We don't really get on.'

'You see them, though?' Pauline asked, tearing her eyes from the family disaster unfolding on the television screen, to the real live one in her living room.

'I see them every couple of weeks, or at least once a month,' Lorna said. 'They live in Glasgow, I'm in the country.' She gave a thin smile. 'It works better that way.'

'You should try and patch things up,' Pauline said. 'You only get one set of parents.'

'We have *patched* things up.' Lorna shrugged. A fortnightly or monthly visit and a weekly chat on the phone was progress, though she wasn't about to tell Pauline that. Or that's how things had been till she'd told them she was staying with James. Her mother had rung her only once since the revelation, talking in low, urgent whispers and insisting she move out, while her father, just as he had all those years ago, refused to even come to the phone.

'And what about work?'

'I should be able to go back the following week.' Lorna yawned and answered at the same time. 'Or definitely the next.'

'So you're not going to look in London?'

'I don't think so.' Lorna gave a tired smile. 'It didn't exactly work out as I planned. If it hadn't been for James I don't know how I'd have managed. Maybe I'm best staying put, where I've got my friends and support.' She was so tired now she didn't finish, just lay there half watching the TV before dozing off. She did not notice when Pauline tucked a throw rug around her and flicked off the TV before heading home to her own family. It was a lovely late afternoon sleep, and that was how James found her when he came home a couple of hours later. His plan had been to stay at work for as long as he could—but, given the hours he'd put in these past weeks, when the usually busy department had suddenly emptied, his loaded in-box was done and sorted, when May, on a late shift, had walked past his office and questioned why he was still there, he really couldn't justify it.

'Go home,' May had scolded. 'No doubt we'll call you back the second you get there, but for now just go home.'

It felt like home as he climbed the steps to his townhouse, and that was what troubled him. He knew she was in there, and the wave of nostalgia that hit him almost knocked this strong man off his feet. The house was in semi-darkness as he walked in with take-away in hand. Lorna, too thin and too pale, was dozing on the sofa, wearing his clothes. It was so like it had once been it almost killed him to see it again.

'Hey!' As she stirred he held up the white plastic bags. 'I stopped and grabbed some Thai.'

'Yum!' She sat up far more easily than she had in recent days and went and got the plates. James opened and served up the food. They sat on the sofa and ate off their knees, Lorna drinking her blackcurrant juice as James enjoyed a glass of red wine. Lorna felt as if she was finally back in contact with the real world. She told James she'd read the paper, seen the news and rung her friends to catch up.

'Not bad for a day's work!' he teased.

'You didn't have to waste your Friday night with me,' Lorna said, when they'd finished their take-away and it was still only eight-thirty. 'I'm sure you've got loads of things to do.'

'Well, you go home on Sunday.' He shrugged.

'Still, I don't need a babysitter, and you get so

little time off—you should be spending it with Ellie. Is she away? Only I haven't seen her.' She took a sip of her blackcurrant juice and found she was holding it in her mouth when he answered.

'We broke up.' James said, rather too lightly.

'I'm sorry.'

'No need to be—it had been on the cards for ages.' He was flicking through the TV channels and something caught his attention. 'Oh, it's…' He stopped then because it was her favourite movie or it had been her favourite movie and he'd liked it too, but for ten years now, whenever it had come on, whenever he'd seen it at the video store, he'd just ignored it.

'I haven't seen it in ages,' Lorna said, so he left it on, but she wished he hadn't. It reminded her of when a sex scene came on the television while her parents were in the room. Even a steamy kiss had had her mother sitting rigid as her father silently fumed— not that there was much sex in this movie, and not that James was rigid or fuming, it was just too close for comfort, a movie that divorced couples should watch alone. It was too late to admit it, so they both sat in a strained silence as they watched two friends who should always have been lovers resisting it at every turn.

He could smell her hair. Even from the other end of the sofa, he always had been able to the night she'd washed it. It was just so thick and long and there was so much of it that the fragrance hung in the air. The only difference was it smelt of his shampoo tonight, instead of her usual. The other difference was that he couldn't reach over and touch it. Actually, not so different, James thought with a rueful smile because by the end of their marriage he hadn't been able to touch it either. Her hand would come up and push his away—as if it made her skin crawl for him to even touch her.

She wouldn't push his hand away tonight. He knew, just knew, that sex hung in the air. It was like trying to breathe deeply in a sauna. There were just a few inches separating them and a whole ten years too, and now she was crying.

He could hear her sniffing. Even though the film was still funny, she always cried at this point because, Lorna had once explained, she knew what was coming, knew what was about to happen.

He'd known her so well and then suddenly he'd found he didn't know her at all.

'What happened to us, Lorna?'

'Please, don't, James,' Lorna said, because she couldn't bear it. She wanted to turn to him like a flower to the sun, to curl up in his lap and let him stroke her hair as they watched the movie, or to lie on the sofa wrapped in his arms and not worry about the ending, only she couldn't. 'Please, don't start about that.'

Except he had to, because there had been no final row, no harsh words, no goodbye sex. He couldn't, though he'd tried and tried to remember, still he couldn't recall the last time they'd made love. He hadn't known that night or day or whenever it had been, that it had been the last time he'd hold her.

'You just left.'

'James.'

'If we could have talked…'

'What was there to say?' Amber eyes met his for the first time since the film had started. 'You told me you felt trapped, that you weren't in love with me.'

'I didn't say that.'

'Yes, James you did. You married me because I was pregnant and then six weeks later I wasn't.' She stood up, didn't care that the film was not quite finished because she knew the ending already, just as she'd known this moment was coming and she couldn't face it. 'I'm tired.'

'Lorna, please…' He stood up, went to take her hands but he took her arms, could feel them thin and rigid beneath his fingers, this little guarded woman who had always confused him and always, always entranced him. 'I just wish we could talk.'

'I can't.'

'Okay,' he said, because that had been the rule. She hadn't asked to come back into his life, circumstance had seen to that. 'You don't have to say anything.' It hurt to let her arms go. Was it so wrong to want to hold her? Was it wrong to take her in his arms? 'Go to bed, we've got our shopping expedition tomorrow.'

She nodded, wiped away the tears with the back of her hand and, as always, she confused him.

''Night, James.' She kissed him on the cheek, which people often did, except they'd avoided it till yesterday. It was just a little kiss, tentative and faltering, but a kiss all the same. The bitter-sweet contact was *dangerous,* but instead of scuttling off to bed, there she stood.

''Night, Lorna.' He meant it, he really meant it, because he'd already given more of himself tonight than he had ever intended. He had told her about Ellie, had pushed her to talk and she'd refused, just as she had after they'd lost the baby, just as she had in that hellish year after the break-up when she'd refused all contact. Now she stood there just a kiss away and he wasn't sure he could go there again and live to tell the tale. He could feel where her lips had been on his cheek, could feel her in his space. Maybe if he kissed her it would be enough, could be the conclusion he'd sought all those years ago. Maybe *this* could be the moment he remembered when in the future he pondered *them* again.

Kiss me. She wouldn't say it, wouldn't kiss him again, but every cell in her body screamed it, and the cries were heeded because his mouth did find hers. For Lorna, the bliss of familiar lips on hers bought a shock of comfort. Shock, because every nerve jumped as their master flicked the switch and declared he was home. Comfort, because his kiss had been sought but never found in others.

It was their *lazy* kiss.

They'd had lots of different types of kisses, but this was their lovely lazy one. Slow and languid and relishing each other, in no rush to move on or retreat, savouring, and how they savoured. She could feel the tears on her cheeks, tasted them too as they ran onto her lips. He tasted them too. They kissed her salty river of tears with their tongues, and breathed each other's air with their mouths. His arms were the nicest place in the whole wide world. He created this little island where it was only the two of them and nothing else mattered. They both pulled back, stared at each other for the longest time, indecision, lust, regret and want all offering differing directions, but there was only one safe road to take and it was James who guided them.

''Night, Lorna.' He kissed her on the cheek, let her go and for three full seconds she stood before turning.

''Night, James.'

CHAPTER TWELVE

FOR a man, he *was* good to shop with.

Or maybe it was that *anything* would look better than the leggings, a rugby shirt and a pair of pumps that Pauline had leant her for the day trip. She also had a scarf and one of his jackets, which meant within minutes of entering a department store she was boiling and had to peel off the layers. It was the quickest shop in history. She bought jeans, a pale grey jumper and the softest beige flat boots that were, even James agreed, divine, and a little holdall to carry the other odd things she'd collected during her time here. Then they were done and sat in the food hall with coffee and cake and, unlike the other frazzled couples around them, not a bicker in sight!

'When did you get so easy?'

'Only with you!'

'I meant…' He didn't try to explain, he'd been trying so hard not to go there, to forget that kiss had even happened. He would choose perhaps to remember it later when she was safely home, but there was a flirty edge to her that no one else could ever see. It had always entranced him, she was such a prim thing, so staid and controlled, but not with him. It was almost as if the Lorna he saw, the Lorna she became around him, was a version reserved exclusively for him. Or it had been in the early days, and here it was again. There was a sort of zing between them that just kept popping up like one of those stupid frog games at the fairground—the harder he hit them down, the faster they popped back up. She looked fantastic today. Oh, she was dressed like an oddball, but it wasn't her clothes he was looking at, it was her hair, her mouth, her eyes, her hands cupping her drink. He wanted to get the hell out of there, for tomorrow to come and Lorna to be gone, so why, oh, why, was his head going to ridiculous places?

'I've got a proposal for you,' he said a few minutes later.

'We tried that once and it didn't work.'

'I'm well aware of that.' James was serious now. 'We need a doctor and you need a job.'

'I think that might be pushing things.'

'So do I.' James nodded. 'However, there are only eight weeks of the rotation left. A couple of our interns dropped out, we're horribly short and we haven't a hope of filling the vacancies so late. We're making do with locums. Now, if you had a couple of weeks off to recover, well, there's six weeks' work for you—albeit as a house officer but you'd get the experience of a busy emergency department. I'm sure you'd have no problem getting snapped up afterwards anywhere you wanted.'

'I don't know if I could work with you, James.' It was important to be honest. 'I

couldn't live with you,' she said, then winced.
'That sounded terrible.'

'No!' James shook his head. 'There was absolutely no offence taken—you are *not* living
with me.'

'Good.'

'Good,' James said. 'But as for working with
me—there isn't time for awkwardness there
and I'm certainly not going to single you out.
We really are desperate for staff.'

'Really?'

'We are.' James nodded, then admitted a
touch more of the truth. 'Okay, maybe it will
be a bit awkward at first, but we'll soon work
it out. So will you think about it?'

'Once I get home,' Lorna agreed.

'Just email me over your résumé for Admin's
sake, so that it looks like a formal application,
and once I've got that we'll take it from there.
There's a job for you if you want it.'

'And if you change your mind,' Lorna
offered, 'if once I'm gone you realise that it

might be a bit much working with me, then just say.'

'I wouldn't say.' James grinned. 'I'd just text or email you.'

He headed back to the counter to get them more coffee and Lorna sat watching his lovely bum as he pushed the tray along the counter, watching how he made the lady who was serving laugh with something he had said, how his dark brown suede jacket had to strain over his broad shoulders and thinking *how much* she wanted to be back in those arms again.

Just one more time.

Just one more night of feeling like a woman before her operation. Six weeks would bring her almost up to her scheduled operation date, not that she could tell him that.

It was hot. She pushed up the sleeves on her rugby shirt, tried not to think about what lay ahead, but it was there all the same. That horrible date in her calendar that only her closest friend knew about.

It was why she'd chosen to move to London. Edinburgh, Glasgow—big cities they may be, except the hospital worlds were small. There was always someone who knew her, or someone who knew her family…her family, who she had chosen not to tell.

If she took up James's offer, in a few weeks she would have the experience she needed to start her life over once she'd had the operation.

Oh, she was *only* having a hysterectomy. It was a completely straightforward procedure, she'd be back at work within a few weeks, ready to embrace life without the roller-coaster of pain—only she'd be minus her womb.

She could easily have dealt with it, if she'd had children. She must deal with it, because she didn't want to fall into the big black hole she'd fallen into after she'd lost the baby.

Their baby.

Lorna forced a smile as he came back over with their coffee, then swallowed as their eyes met for an indecent second. She managed a genuine smile, though, as he slopped half the coffee into the saucers. She'd spent two-thirds of her life avoiding problems, keeping the peace, not making waves, he just hadn't known her for the last third.

The last third was where she'd hauled herself out of the black hole, stood up to her parents and become the woman she had almost managed to become with James. The woman who had always been there, waiting for her to assert herself, a woman who dealt with things instead of hoping they would just go away.

And without facing the undeniable attraction that was flaring now, without dealing with it head on, it wasn't going to go away.

'About me working with you—well, we have a problem we need to discuss.'

Okay, it was time, Lorna decided, time to live that life of no regrets. Oh, and there would be regrets if she didn't make herself say it now. Lorna knew that, could almost see herself lying on the gurney pre-op and wishing that day they'd gone shopping she'd found it within herself to be brave. One more night, Lorna told herself. It was certainly an incentive to push on.

She *would* be brave.

'I've told you—it might be awkward at first.'

'It could be a lot less awkward…' Lorna gave up with her coffee and replaced it in her saucer. 'I think we ought to clear the air.'

'Talk, you mean?' James frowned when she shook her head.

'No, not talk. There's a sudden awkwardness between us,' Lorna croaked. 'You remember that kiss…' She could see his tongue rolling around in his cheek, knew that his silence didn't mean he wasn't hearing her. 'Do you know what I'm talking about?'

'I think so.' He was looking at her and she felt as if he was peeling off her skin. Four knees under the table were neatly divided into two and cramp was almost setting in from the effort of keeping them still. 'We didn't work out…' She waited till he nodded. 'We can't ever go back.'

'I know that,' James agreed, his mind telling him she was right, his heart disinclined to follow, but then he remembered the rows, the hurt, the pit they had both fallen into, and after a moment's consideration his heart reluctantly accepted the fact.

'But.' Lorna took a deep breath.

'But?' The tables really were too small, because there was slight contact. They didn't both jump, they very deliberately stayed still and silent for a second, waiting for the scales to adjust and settle, before slowly tipping them again.

'There were some good bits.' How she was managing to look at him was a mystery, except she was. She could see a muscle flicker in his cheek, feel just a little bit more of his knee on hers, and she wanted to put her hand there, to slide it up his solid thigh and do away with words. But they were needed, because this was important, too important not to make things clear from the start or, rather, Lorna thought, the end. 'There were also a lot of not-so-good bits,' she said, thinking of the sad demise of their wonderful sex life. That glorious part of them had been so rapidly reduced to Saturdays when he wasn't working or she wasn't deep in a book, studying, and birthdays and duty sex. 'The thing is,' Lorna croaked, 'I've always regretted that I can't remember the last time we did it.'

'It?' James checked.

'It.' Lorna nodded.

She saw his eyes widen, the shock of recognition in them that told her he'd thought exactly the same. 'Neither can I.'

'I can remember lots of *times,*' Lorna said carefully, 'lots of really fantastic times. I just can't remember the last time and I wish sometimes that I could.'

'Me too.'

'We could make a new *last time.*'

He'd been wandering in the woods for weeks now and suddenly here he was, only it wasn't a gingerbread house he'd found but a red-headed woman he could feast on again, just one more time, end it on a high, instead of the crushing low that had been hell for both of them to crawl back from.

'We could say goodbye properly,' Lorna pushed, 'because it would be goodbye, James. I mean, if I come and work in London, I *will* be your ex…'

'You have to be, Lorna,' James agreed, 'because I can't go through it again.'

'I know,' she said, because she did and she wouldn't put him through it again, wouldn't give the man who deserved so much more this half-woman with a childless future, and the goody bag of depression that was sure to follow her surgery.

She promised herself right there in the food hall that she wouldn't do it to him and she wouldn't do it to them. No, this was the twenty-first century, people, ex-lovers, friends did things like this all the time—and it was James she was suggesting it to, James who had always looked after her in that way, James, the only man she had ever really been able to be completely herself with.

Good and bad.

'One night,' Lorna said, warmed by the prospect and desperate to get the hell out of the food hall. 'One lovely, lovely night.'

'That we can look back on.' He laughed as she smiled that old wicked smile. Sometimes he could read her mind before she'd even thought something, as if they were one person who shared the same thoughts.

'No photos! Lorna feigned horror. 'What sort of woman do you think I am?'

That seemed funny and witty at the time, but as they walked through the shop and to the car park all she felt was stupid and horribly, horribly nervous—having offered him a night of fabulous sex, suddenly she wasn't so sure she was up to the job. When they finally got to the car he gave her her answer. He had to hold her so suddenly that he didn't even have time to open the door. He pressed her against it, his lips crushing hers, and mindful of her chest, ever the gentleman, he wrapped her in his arms and wedged her to the metal with another part of his anatomy. He kissed her till she wanted to climb into his skin, wanted to crawl under his coat. It was their *taxi* kiss this time, the one where it would be almost impossible to drive, so either they had to run into a hotel, or, as they'd once done, call a taxi because James wouldn't have been able to keep his hands on the wheel for the ride home.

'The best sort of woman,' he said, answering her question from a while ago between kisses, oblivious to the other shoppers. He kissed her till for decency's sake he bundled her in the car and took her home.

CHAPTER THIRTEEN

THE trouble with reunion sex, Lorna decided as they fell through the front door, tearing at each other's faces with their mouths, is that you *know* how the other likes it. On the rather rapid drive home she'd fleetingly wondered if they'd run a bath, or make slow blissful tender love, but when he stalled the car, reversing it into his rather small parking spot and then forgot to put his handbrake on and she had to remind him, Lorna was quietly delighted that that would all come later—after all, they had the whole night.

The trouble with condoms, Lorna also decided as he kissed her into the hall, was that nice guys, which James was, didn't suddenly whip one from their wallet, one that they'd been carrying just in case. Oh, she knew where they were, she'd seen them when she'd been rummaging in his bathroom, except the stairs looked like Mount Everest all of a sudden and her oxygen levels were somewhat depleted as he pulled his rugby shirt off her and she kicked off her shoes, and James shrugged out of his jacket.

They did *try*, Lorna reasoned as she sank to her knees, a pile of clothes strewn in their wake…

'Oh, Lorna.'

He was taking off her bra now, kissing the little breasts she'd always hated so, but that James had adored. Their little buds swelled in his lips and beneath his fingers as, spoiled for choice, he greeted them both. His shirt was off but she couldn't remember removing it. She ran her hands along his familiar shoulders and then slipped them under his arms. Her long, cold fingers checked every rib, every vertebra as her mouth moved over his broad shoulder. It took only seconds—just a few seconds to familiarise her fingers, her mouth, her skin with the delicious planes of his body. They might have made it up the stairs had she not found his belt, wrestled with the heavy leather, tried to get his trousers down. It was rather awkward while he was kneeling, so he stood and dispensed with the clothing as Lorna attempted the final summit, but then he caught her ankle and the attempt was thwarted, the climb happily abandoned.

James, four steps down, was kissing her deeply *there,* her legs wrapped around his head and her fingers tugging at his hair, his lovely soft hair, and his big thick arms that held her buttocks as his hands spanned her waist. It was James, and it was bliss, and she couldn't stop crying, and she couldn't stop saying his name, because that was what he did to her. He pulled at every emotion buried inside her and exposed it, took all guilt and shame and erased it, because if this beautiful man wanted her so much, so very, very much, then surely it had to be good, and with James it was.

It just was.

And she'd miss him for ever.

She could hear him moaning, and that told her before she even knew it that she was going to come, because he knew her body better than her. She wanted him inside her, didn't want to do it alone, so she was tugging at his head, dragging that lovely body up to her level.

'Are you on the Pill?' He had a lovely dewy look in his eyes, a lusty, almost drunk look that drove her to delicious distraction. In this trance-like state he struggled to deal with the practicalities, but luckily Lorna had already dealt with them, long ago.

'Yes!'

She was on the Pill, she was on hundreds of bloody pills, in fact, but she told him only about the one that mattered, only the one that he needed to know about today.

'Yes!' She was pleading, begging, urgent. 'Yes!' She wept as he swept into her, and she welcomed him with tight, tight hugs, a sweet frantic release as he groaned, as he took her to a place, a white-noise place that drowned out everything, took her back to their little island where it was only the two of them and nothing and no one could touch them.

'The best,' he said, kissing her with a kiss she didn't have a name for yet, laced with tenderness and regret and something else she couldn't find the word for, but she'd work that one out later.

And then the night was just for them—and them alone—back in his bedroom closing the door on the world, shutting it all away as they slowly kissed each other goodbye.

CHAPTER FOURTEEN

'I HAVE to get away by midday.' Pauline surveyed the bomb site that was the kitchen on the following Monday morning. The surfaces were littered with mugs and champagne glasses and the scent of debauchery was in the air. Not that you could tell from looking at him. Not that you could ever tell from looking at him! Clean shaven, he was wearing one of those blessed linen shirts that took for ever for her to iron and chomping on his toast. Butter wouldn't have melted in his mouth as he sat reading the paper.

'No problem.'

'I might not get it all done.' She bobbed her head into the lounge, which unfortunately was the only decent room in the place; she'd been hoping to tackle it today because there was a show she wanted to watch at eleven. Still, he had pay TV in his room, Pauline reminded herself. 'I'll do your bedroom after the kitchen. Give it a good spring clean now that Lorna's gone.'

'Actually…' James stood up and attempted to find his keys. 'Could you leave the bedroom? I started doing my tax return last night, there are papers everywhere. Don't even go in.' He flashed her a smile. 'I've got a pile of receipts.'

Work was busy, which for James was good— anything to take his mind off her. He immersed himself in the rhythm of the busy department. A cyclist hit by a taxi got him through to eight forty-five a.m. before the trauma team took over his case. A jogger with a dislocated patella was a quick distraction. James popped it back while the patient was still on the stretcher. That got him to nine a.m. Then there was a meeting in Admin. He did try to focus, but his foot kept tapping and he kept having to ask the CEO if he'd mind repeating the question.

'I wasn't asking a question,' Brent Gillard said tartly. 'I was *stating* that the delays have been far too long in your department in recent weeks.'

'Because we're two doctors down,' James answered back. 'Because the consultants and registrars are dealing with the stuff that the SHOs usually do.'

'We've provided locums,' Brent responded coolly.

'Just never the same one twice.' James's tone would have cut ice. 'Which means they have to be orientated, which means they don't even know where the IV trolley is, or the patella hammer, or how to use the paging system... I could go on.'

'Please don't.' Brent said. 'Just get the waiting times down.'

James was not best pleased when he strode back into Emergency, especially when May followed him into his office.

'I don't care if this is a bad time!' May slammed the door closed in a way only a very good colleague could, but he was boiling too, refusing to look at her, refusing to respond, lest he say the wrong thing. He flicked through his emails as May ranted on. 'I have just had another locum *shouting* at one of *my* nurses because she dared to buzz him on his coffee-break. I tell you, James, this place is at breaking point. Something has to give.'

'It just did.' James looked up at his favourite nurse. 'I quit!'

'No!' May practically shrivelled in front of him. 'No, James.'

'Er, I was joking!'

'Cheeky pup.'

'Remember Dean Hayes?'

'The one with the terrible dandruff?' May frowned as she placed him.

'That's him.' James nodded. 'Well, he's jetting off to Europe in two months and has emailed asking for every shift available.'

'He is good.' May nodded, but was only slightly mollified.

'And Lorna.' James cleared his throat. 'She just sent in her résumé. She can start in two weeks, light duties only, but she's very good, very sharp.'

'She's a GP, isn't she?'

'She is—and she also covers a rural area, so she's pretty used to dealing with whatever lands in her lap, though she might struggle with the volume.'

'She'll cope.'

'And I'll go and have a word with the locum.'

'Right!' May gave him a very nice smile. 'That is better!'

'I'll email Dean and give him a pile of work.' He gave a shrug. 'I'll ring Admin now and tell them I've just done a telephone interview with Lorna. I know it's been hard on the nursing staff…'

'We'll get there.' May smiled. 'Okay, I'll give the girls the news and then I'm off.'

'It's only midday.'

'Ah, but I'm on the old contract.' May smiled. 'And I'm glad that I dug my heels in—I still get my half-days!'

That took him to midday, but all he wanted to do was go home, all he wanted to do was remember. He had no qualms about Pauline cleaning up behind him, he'd long since stopped feeling embarrassed when he'd come home to find a neat little pile of earrings and bras that she'd retrieved during her working day. He no longer noticed the way her mouth disappeared into itself when a pretty new face tumbled into the kitchen as she was unloading the dishwasher.

He wanted his room as Lorna had left it— wanted the scent of her in the bedroom and a couple of long auburn hairs on his bathroom floor for just a little while longer—*then* he'd deal with getting over her.

Again.

CHAPTER FIFTEEN

'His tax return?' May lowered the elevation on her treadmill so she was walking on flat ground at two miles an hour. 'He's doing his tax return at this time of the year?'

'He's got papers everywhere,' Pauline huffed, still climbing up that hill, 'apparently.'

'Apparently?'

'I'm not to open the door in case it disturbs his receipts.'

They stopped talking for a minute, first to get their breath back and second, to ponder the lovely young man who was working on his pectorals.

'I did pop in to say goodbye to Lorna,' Pauline added fifteen minutes later as they rewarded their workout with croissants and cappuccinos.

'It would have been so lovely to see her before she went, but I didn't have the heart to disturb them, they were up in his bedroom.'

'In his bedroom, you say?'

'She was crying.' Pauline said, discreetly *not* mentioning the underwear strewn banister that had greeted her along with the thuds from the bedroom. 'Up in her room, well, his room, but she's used it since she was there. It has a bathroom, you see.'

'Well, that makes sense.' May nodded. 'She was crying, you say?'

'Sobbing actually,' Pauline confirmed, pursing her lips and catching May's eyes. 'It would break the coldest heart to hear it—it's good that he was there.' She took a bite of her croissant. 'To comfort her, of course.'

'Poor pet,' May tutted, then rallied. 'Did I mention she was coming back?'

CHAPTER SIXTEEN

SHE was just a colleague.

Over and over he told himself that as he skimmed through her résumé.

She was also his ex-wife, James consoled himself as he read it more closely, as every detail was imprinted for ever on his mind.

It was natural to be curious.

Natural to notice that she'd now become an organ donor and that her hobbies were listed as swimming, tennis and triathalon.

Liar, liar, liar James had wanted to respond to her, but he fired it over to Admin and sent a quick email to her headed 'Reading, reading, reading', which he knew she'd understand. That was the only hobby he'd ever seen her indulging in! Then he sat back, watching as his past developed into the present.

The security check cleared, and then in came her new London address, which meant that she was already here in London. Then her certificate check came through too.

It was a slow process and one he was entirely used to. Then the thick envelope arrived—the one he couldn't open—with her medical details that were sealed and had to go straight to Admin. It contained her past medical history. It infuriated him that the ectopic pregnancy would be in her notes but not in his. It had hurt him just as much, but apparently it didn't count.

Oh, but it did.

He'd *told* her to sign the consent form. In bitter truthfulness with himself, James admitted that in the end he'd been impatient with her. He'd had to be firm with her. The registrar had taken him aside and told him there was no way the baby could survive and if they delayed and the pregnancy ruptured, yes, they were in a big hospital and they would be onto it straight away, but there would be serious risks involved.

'Just sign the form, Lorna.' Ten years on he could still recall the expression on her face when he'd pushed her to get on with the inevitable—a mixture of grief, hurt, trust and hate, as her shaky hand had taken the pen from him. They'd wheeled her off to Theatre some five minutes later, and there had been a sense of foreboding inside him as he'd sat in the waiting room, watching the clock.

He'd known they'd lost the baby, but somehow he'd also lost *them*. That dark thought had been confirmed when she'd come to after the operation. She had removed her hand from his and then rolled on her side and faced the curtain. In a particularly cruel twist, the female ward had been under refurbishment, so she had only been a corridor away from Maternity—babies' cries carried at night.

'Lorna, talk to me.' Over and over he said it, hoping things would improve once they got home, except they didn't. It felt like two strangers waking up after a wild party to find they had nothing in common except for the mess and the misery they had both created.

There *were* certain privileges to being a doctor, however.

If you could call them that.

James was able to call up the results from that little jar neatly labelled 'POC' that had headed off to the lab. He could still remember crawling into bed and holding Lorna's taut, skinny body, trying to imbue some warmth into her, desperate to hold her, to scoop her into his arms and cry with her.

Except Lorna was in a different place.

A dark, lonely place where she did not want him beside her.

But he was lonely too—holding that knowledge inside him, getting up to go to the loo at two a.m. and wanting to kick the door.

His little Product of Conception—or POC because it was too long to write on the label—

had been their baby, a little girl, their daughter, and he'd never told Lorna that, because surely it was easier not to know.

He missed his daughter.

He missed Lily—Lily Morrell, it was the name they had decided on for a girl, and *how* he missed her.

Not every minute, not even every day—but even ten years on, *still* he missed that amber-eyed brunette or that green-eyed redhead, or that black-haired, black-eyed girl they might just have made. This little puzzle of genes and personality that hadn't clicked into place—he still rued the card that fate had dealt them and still he mourned that glimpse of fatherhood.

Who, James thought as he shoved the envelope into its pigeonhole and sent it on its way to the nameless faces in Admin, said that men had it easy?

CHAPTER SEVENTEEN

'HEY.' They met for coffee the day before she started work.

Nice neutral territory, they sat on the sofa and there were no pressing knees. There was no real awkwardness this time, it was just good to see each other.

'You look really well.' She did. She'd put on some weight. Oh, she was still way too thin and too pale, but there was a lightness to her, a breeze of good health that surrounded her as she accepted her coffee and took a long sip.

'I feel it.' Lorna smiled. 'Mind you, I could do with another week off. Not for my health,' she added quickly, 'it's just been so busy, finding somewhere to live, getting everything out of storage and moving it down.'

'Making lots of lists,' James teased.

'Oh, there were plenty of lists,' Lorna assured him, and then she admitted a little of the truth. 'I am nervous.'

'I know.'

'I know I can deal with the patients, I know I'm qualified, it's just the volume of patients.'

'There are way more staff too, though,' James pointed out. 'You won't be on your own for a minute. There's always a registrar on, twenty-four hours a day. Even at night the consultants are often there. You saw yourself how many times I got called in. It will take a few days, but by the end of the week you'll be an old hand.'

'I doubt it,' Lorna said, not caring that effectively it was her boss she was admitting her insecurities to. He also happened to be James!

'How do you think your colleagues will be?

I mean, I guess they all know that I'm your ex-wife.'

'They'll be curious,' James admitted. 'And Abby, she's a registrar and she might be a bit standoffish. She's got a thing for me.'

'A lot of women do.' Lorna smiled, because now she could smile about it. When they had first started going out and in the hellish months of their marriage it had made her feel insecure. It had taken for ever to work out that James rarely noticed the effect he had on women, so for him to have noticed that Abby liked him meant a nose would be seriously out of joint. 'Have you gone out with her?' she asked, not to be nosy, but forewarned was forearmed and a registrar with ex-husband envy wasn't something Lorna was looking forward to dealing with.

'No.' James shook his head. 'I never go out with people from work.'

'Never?' Lorna checked, because before *she*

had gone out with him, James had always had someone on the go. 'Since when?'

'Since I learnt my lesson with you.'

'This is going to be so awkward for you.' Lorna winced, but James just shrugged.

'I don't see why—as long as we're not awkward around each other. Also...' He cleared his throat for a moment before continuing and Lorna could tell he was a touch uncomfortable. 'I don't really discuss my private life with them,' James explained. 'Which is ironic, given that my private life is what everyone is talking about right now. I haven't advertised the fact that I've broken up with Ellie.'

Lorna frowned.

'So...' he was just a touch pink around his ears '...I'm assuming people will be thinking that if Ellie's okay with you working there, then there really can't be anything going on between us. Which there isn't, of course!' he quickly added.

'Of course,' Lorna agreed, because there wasn't.

He paid for the coffee, and this time it was without thought or innuendo that they kissed each other on the cheek. They were friends now, good friends even.

They were exes James reminded himself, as she clipped down the street in high black boots and a massive blonde coat, gorgeous now she was wearing her own clothes. Exes who had said their goodbyes in the nicest possible way and had cleared the air, if not his head.

There was, of course, a huge wave of curiosity that swept through the department.

James Morrell's ex-wife was coming to work there, and there was a morbid curiosity that awaited her at every shift change during her first couple of weeks. The staff were sure Lorna and James must be an item, and if Lorna was James's ex, she must be pretty spectacular.

She soon put paid to rumour.

Dressed in grey or sombre brown suits, her glasses perched on her nose, her skinny legs wrapped in forty-denier stockings, her hair scraped back, she was neurotic to a fault about obs charts and drove the junior staff to the edge of irritation and beyond.

'She's awful,' said Shona as they waited for Lorna to write up her orders, her neat handwriting, her detailed note-taking slowing everything down. 'She just doesn't get it.'

'Doesn't get what?' May frowned.

'She's so slow,' Shona sighed. 'Double checking everything, even what we do!'

'She's just so *awkward,*' Lavinia agreed, 'so obsessive.'

Which she was. Maybe the other hospitals had been right to reject her, Lorna thought over and over throughout that first horrible couple of weeks. There were just so many things to think of, so many names to get to know and so few familiar faces. There was May, of course, the lovely Irish nurse, and there was James.

She was horribly awkward around him. Aware the emergency world was watching them, she avoided him like the plague but of course, she couldn't avoid him completely. She watched her own hand shake as she tried to put in an IV on a rowdy drunk who refused to stay still. Of course she missed the vein.

James didn't offer to do it for her, left her to deal with the expletives from the patient, which was par for the course in this place. But James felt like a worried parent, waving his child off to school each morning. And Lorna was like a child that didn't want to go, a child that didn't quite fit in, while James had to pretend he was okay with it, that everything was going to be just fine. He couldn't help her, couldn't do it for her, and he couldn't show her he was worried. All he *could* do was wiggle the roster a little without anyone knowing to make sure she was, as far as possible, always on with May, and just hold his breath.

* * *

'Happy birthday!' James kissed her on the cheek as she walked into the tapas bar and took her seat beside him at the little bench table.

'Thanks a lot!' Lorna groaned. 'I can't believe you'd put me on a night shift on my birthday.'

'We agreed no favours.' James grinned. 'And you didn't put in a request for the night off.'

They couldn't talk at work because everyone was watching them, and it didn't feel right to go to each other's homes, so they met for supper one evening before her night shift started, which just happened to be her birthday.

He could have lied and said that he'd forgotten it was her birthday but, well, they'd have both known he was lying. In fact, James's hand had hovered over the keyboard as he'd typed in the shifts because, given she was alone in London and it was her birthday, he was quite sure he'd have ended up taking her out.

He had ended up taking her out, James

thought ruefully as he ordered himself a soft drink because he was on call and Lorna a lemonade because she was working. But it was only supper and, given she started work at nine, there was no danger there!

'Here.' He handed her a small package and Lorna frowned as she took it, wondering what on earth an ex-husband bought an ex-wife on her birthday.

'A chain for my glasses?'

'You can never find them.'

'But *old* people have them—the guys at work already think I'm dowdy enough.'

'I think they'll suit you!' James shrugged.

'When did you develop a librarian fetish?' She stopped then. They both took a quick swig of their drinks as way too easily they slipped into talk of old. They ordered their tapas and told each other they were definitely *not* going to talk about work, but with flirting off the agenda, and their past not open to inspection, it really didn't make for sparkling conversation—what *was* there to talk about?

'How's Pauline?'

'Good. She's doing a Thai cooking course.' James sighed. 'I *used* to like Thai.'

Which dealt with that.

'What happened with the car insurance?'

'All sorted,' Lorna said brightly. 'Not that I really need a car here.'

'Well, it will be good for driving home.'

'I'll stick with the tube,' Lorna said, which killed that conversation stone dead.

'It's not working, Lorna,' James said, three long, silent minutes later, and watched the colour whoosh up her pale cheeks and knew she understood what he was saying. 'Goodbye sex might be good in theory and it might work for some, but all it's done for me is remind me how good we were. And,' he added, 'I'm not talking just about the sex.'

'I know.' He could see the tip of her nose

redden, as it always did when she was about to cry.

'We've never really dated.' James said. 'We've never done this…'

'I know.' She was rubbing the bridge of her nose with her thumb and finger and James wished she'd look at him. 'It wouldn't work…' she shook her head. 'Not with us working together.'

'Fair enough.' James nodded. 'But when you finish up, maybe if you get a job in London…'

'We can't.'

'Lorna!' James was annoyed now. 'We're crazy about each other and, yes, it might annoy your parents—'

'It has nothing to do with my parents,' Lorna interrupted him. 'Will you stop assuming I'm the same as I was back then?'

'What, then?' James demanded. 'What's stopping us from trying?'

'Because it didn't work.'

'Because you refused to talk to me—you chose to shut me out.'

'I'd lost a baby.'

'You'd lost my baby, Lorna.' The sight of deep-fried olives was making her stomach curl, this conversation was too close to such a very raw wound. 'I was devastated too. You know how much I wanted that baby, how much I wanted to have children.'

'Just leave it, please!'

And he did, at that moment, ten years on, in a bar in London, James finally left the relationship. He didn't stop loving and he'd never stop caring, but in that moment he accepted the facts because, as she'd repeatedly said, *they* didn't work. Her pinched face, the trauma he inflicted when he asked for a piece of her. Finally James accepted it was something she chose not to give.

'Please just leave it, James. We can't go back.'

'I know,' he said, because now he did, because all it did was hurt. Because here she was crying on her birthday and as always it was him feeling like a bastard for pushing her, and it shouldn't be this way. 'You're right, Lorna, we can't go back.'

And she gulped a bit when he said that, because something in his voice told her he meant it.

'Hey!' He wrapped an arm around her and gave her a serviette to mop up her tears. 'You know it wasn't goodbye sex we needed, it was a good row.' He felt her laugh and cry in his arms. 'To remind us just how bad it could be.'

And it did clear the air—well, sort of.

He walked her to the underground, watched her disappear down the steps and told himself that finally it was over.

He just had to get used to it, that was all.

'Could I have a word please, Lorna?'

Abby called her into her office before Lorna had even taken off her coat. Lorna's head was still spinning from supper with James and walking through the waiting room. The department was already pumping and though there was always a registrar on and a consultant covering, the workload was more intense at night. There were more decisions to be made without consultation and, frankly, Lorna felt sick.

'Are you looking forward to your stint on nights, Lorna?' Abby was smiling as Lorna took a seat.

'Very much so.' Lorna nodded, trying to inject some enthusiasm, trying keep her heart rate even as another siren blared and the blue lights flashed past Abby's high window.

'Well, I'm on tonight and tomorrow too. James is, of course, on call, but naturally I'd prefer that you run things by me before you call him for anything.'

'Absolutely.'

'Obviously…' Abby grinned '…I'm not talking about personal calls.'

'I'll speak with you before I ring James,' Lorna said, gritting her teeth but refusing to explain herself or James to Abby. 'And judging by the waiting room, there won't be much time to make personal calls.'

'It does look busy,' Abby agreed. 'Which is why I wanted to have a word. I know it's awkward with James being your ex. Maybe he doesn't feel he can discuss certain matters with you, which is why I'm going to have a quiet word. Just between us.' Lorna could feel the tears at the back of her eyes as very politely, very nicely, Abby ripped into her. She absolutely refused to cry as she was told how irritated all the staff were with her note-taking, how she had to assert herself more and how she had to stop referring everyone on, instead of making the decision herself to discharge them.

It was quite a list Abby had to get through, but she soldiered on, till by the end of it Lorna felt like a wrung-out dishrag and the night hadn't even started yet.

'You don't have to always do a full examination,' Abby continued as she had for the past twenty minutes. 'And you don't then have to go and spend another fifteen minutes writing up your notes. Not everything ends up in the coroner's court, Lorna. You don't have to constantly cover yourself.'

'I'm not *covering* myself,' Lorna said. 'I admit I am rather slow, but I like to take a thorough history. It's the way I work.'

'In a rural GP setting,' Abby responded. 'Just see if you can pick up the pace a bit, Lorna, that's all I'm asking.'

'I will.' Lorna stood up and politely she said the right thing. 'Thanks for your guidance.'

'Any time.' Abby smiled.

Lorna was tempted to walk out the door, but instead she made a coffee and went and joined the *team* who considered her irritating, and sat quietly among them.

'Are you on nights too?' Lorna's flagging ego soared just a little when May, basket in one hand, mug of tea in the other, walked into the staffroom where the night team were getting ready to start work.

'I am!' May was less than impressed. 'I did a stint last month. Do they think I don't have a bed to get into at night? Stuck in this hellhole on a Friday night, you're about to have your eyes opened, young lady.'

'I know.' Lorna admitted glumly, then rallied. 'I did my rotation in Edinburgh.'

'How many years ago was that?' May did nothing to soothe her. 'They've invented an entire new set of problems now—crack this and meth that, and there's no such thing as closing time now. Last drinks used to be at eleven, that's when they *start* now. Just what do you do all night?' She asked Shona accusingly, as if she were the entire youth problem.

'We dance!' Shona said. Young, gorgeous and minus insecurities, she did a strange spaced-out motion that had every one giggling, even Lorna. 'Like this!'

'That's not dancing!' May jeered. 'This is dancing.' And she took Shona by the hand and spun her round till the whole room was laughing, even Lorna, and she loved them. She loved them all and wanted to fit in, wanted to be one of them, but she could never be so loose with herself and anyway there was no point really, because in a couple of weeks she'd be gone. In a couple of weeks, if she did get a job, if James did put in a word, she'd be in another London hospital and starting all over again.

'Come on, Lorna!' May gave her a very nice smile. 'I'll look after you.'

She certainly did. May, Lorna realised, looked after everyone. She had her finger on every pulse and not just the patients'. She could smell trouble before it even arrived and there was something so stoic about her, something so *right,* that she commanded respect even from those who never usually gave it—because, Lorna worked out, watching her chatting to Rita, a tired sex worker who was holding a wad of gauze to her scalp, May respected them.

And so too did Lorna.

A London A and E brought in a very fresh set of problems—some she recognised, some she didn't, but always Lorna tried.

'It doesn't have to be this way,' she said to Rita at two a.m. when she finally got around to stitching her scalp.

The language that followed defied imagination. May put on the kettle and prepared to mop up tears, but Lorna wasn't crying.

'You can't change the world,' May said.

'No!' A little prim face stared her right in the eye. 'But if she'd let me, I'd change it for her.'

It was rather uplifting when at six a.m. a street-weary face reappeared and asked for the 'posh Scottish doctor'. May duly buzzed Lorna and her pale, sleep-deprived face appeared.

May wasn't privy to what was said. Lorna took two mugs of coffee into the interview room and emerged a good hour later. But as May filled in her time sheet and rinsed her Thermos before placing it in her basket, at some level she knew something good had been done at the crack of dawn—something very good indeed.

Nothing that would change the world, of course, May thought as her beloved husband kissed her hello, her tea and toast waiting just as it always was when she did nights. He kissed her goodbye this morning as he dashed to his own work but May sat in the living room for a quiet moment of reflection before heading off to bed. Yes, something had been done this morning that would hopefully change one person's world.

It was plenty to get to sleep on.

CHAPTER EIGHTEEN

SHE wore her glasses chain. It was actually very useful, even if she did look like a sour old spinster, but she didn't care. No, what Lorna cared about more was when James was called in at eleven on the Saturday night.

'Sorry, James.' She heard Abby call out to him as Lorna sat perched on the end of a gurney in Resus, taking a cardiac history from a recent arrival. 'We've had two stabbings and trauma and the surgeons are all in Theatre. I can't stop this arm bleeding.'

'No problem,' James said, and Abby glanced over, saw him tying a plastic apron over his going-out-on-a-Saturday-night clothes and pulling on some rubber gloves. He nodded over to her, a polite nod, not a hint of suggestiveness, or the teeny wink that he would normally have given, and Lorna knew that the door to his heart was finally closed to her.

'Ellie didn't seem too impressed at me pulling you away.'

For just a second their eyes met, James a touch uncomfortable, Lorna trying to pretend that a six-inch knife hadn't just plunged through her heart.

'Ellie's used to it,' James said. And that, as they say, was that.

Lorna dropped her gaze and carried on taking the patient history. James pulled back the gauze on the arterial bleed and called for the light to be lowered and for a pair of forceps. They did their best to get on with the rest of the night.

'He just needed stitching.' Abby popped her head into the suture theatre later, where Lorna was checking a patient's BP. The place was steaming. A thick pile of white cards was clipped to the theatre door and every one of them was waiting to be sutured.

She'd been working her way through them, trying not to care that James had long since gone, trying not to think about his nice big bed and Ellie in it. She had sutured Mr Devlon's hand wound as Abby had instructed, but just as Lavinia was setting up for the next one, the patient had a dizzy turn as he climbed down off the theatre bed.

'I'll take him to one of the cubicles. He can have a little rest before he goes home.' Lavinia offered, only Lorna wasn't happy with that.

She *had,* even though it had hurt, taken on board Abby's criticism and had picked up speed, trying not to stall on minor details, which was, Lorna admitted to herself, her usual way. She had found out why doctors had a reputation for messy writing as she'd signed her name at the bottom of countless casualty cards and done her very best not to take a lengthy history and then do a full body examination for a straight-forward sprained ankle.

Only it went against her methodical mind—

if the doctor wasn't looking for trouble, then who else would?

And Mr Devlon was a tough man, a carpenter by trade who had, as he'd told her, been stitched more times than he could remember, so why was he looking so grey and about to faint?

'It happens sometimes after stitching.' Lavinia had his head down and was telling him to take deep breaths, and, of course, patients often did feel sick or faint after stitching, Lorna knew *that* much, but there was something about Mr Devlon that didn't seem right to her.

'Pop him into a cubicle,' Lorna said, 'and get him into a gown and I'll come and take a proper look at him.'

'Abby's already examined him,' Lavinia said. 'He's for discharge after stitching.'

'Except he's about to faint.' Lorna was having great difficulty asserting herself, but Abby had told her to after all! 'Just put him in a cubicle, please.'

She could almost feel the daggers Abby was

shooting into her back as she headed for the cubicle, but at three a.m. this Sunday morning, even if she cared, she cared about her patients more. She refused to practise sticky-plaster medicine, just because some registrar told her that was how it should be done!

Lavinia had got him into a gown and, of course, he looked the picture of health now, smiling and joking away to the nurse as Lorna walked in.

'How are you feeling now, Mr Devlon?'

'Grand!' he said. 'I don't know what happened in there.'

'You cut your hand on a Stanley knife?'

'That's right,' he agreed as Lorna skimmed through his brief notes. 'I'm laying a carpet.'

'There was no dizziness?' She watched him hesitate for just a moment before he answered.

'Well, I felt a bit dizzy after,' he admitted, 'but there was quite a bit of blood.' He smiled at Lavinia, who was standing with a rather bored expression on her face, but she smiled nicely back at the patient. 'Got it all over the new carpet. The wife's not going to be too pleased.'

'I'm talking about when you cut yourself,' Lorna said. 'Was there any dizziness prior to that?'

'Well, maybe a bit.' Mr Devlon shrugged. 'I just came over a bit queer.'

'Has that happened before?'

'Nope.'

'Never?' She was chatting away as she examined him, trying to be quick, yet trying not to rush things, sensing Mr Devlon's reluctance and noting it to herself.

'As I said to the other doctor, apart from the odd accident at work, I've never had a day's sickness in my life.'

'Okay.' She'd listened to his chest, had examined him neurologically, and now she lowered the trolley and asked him to lie flat so she could examine his abdomen.

'Have you been feeling well today?'

'A bit off…' He gave a sort of small grimace

as Lorna probed. 'Look, I passed a bit of blood. This evening, before I started on the carpet.'

'Fresh blood?' Lorna checked in a matter-of-fact voice, but Mr Devlon didn't answer. Irritated and restless, he sat up. He took a couple of big breaths but his face was a horrible grey colour again.

'Actually, I need to go to the bathroom.'

'Could you get a pan please, Lavinia?'

Lavinia was about to roll her eyes, of that Lorna was quite sure, but her bored expression quickly changed as she glanced down at the patient. The once ruddy pink Mr Devlon was grey, and sweating profusely, trying to get off the trolley to get to the bathroom as finally the two women worked together.

Lavinia, grabbed a pan from under the trolley and talked calmly to the embarrassed, restless man as Lorna pulled on an oxygen mask.

'It's okay,' Lavinia said, pressing the call bell for assistance. The poor man was lying sweating on the trolley and on the point of collapse as Lorna quickly wrapped a tourniquet around his arm, but Lorna could see her fingers trembling, and knew she was going to miss.

'I'll do it.' Lavinia swiftly nudged her out of the way and completed the procedure as Lorna ran through a drip.

'What have we got?' May dashed in just when she was needed. The patient had collapsed totally and they had him flat on the trolley now, the pan had been taken away, and the head of the bed lowered as they dashed him over to Resus.

'Massive PR bleed,' Lorna responded in a matter-of-fact voice, deliberately not looking at Abby as she joined them in Resus. 'He had one earlier in the evening but was reluctant to say.'

'Isn't that the hand injury?' May could chat and summon the surgeons at the same time. 'I thought he was on his way home.'

Had Abby bothered to try and get to know her better, she'd have known that Lorna wasn't one to gloat—victory was rather hollow when it meant a patient was sick. All Lorna wanted was guidance instead of criticism but, rather than improve matters, if anything it made them worse. Lorna, given what had happened to Mr Devlon, was completely paranoid about all her patients now and slowed down further, if that was possible. Abby, defensive and scornful, took every opportunity to point out that if you worked in Emergency long enough there were always patients that surprised you, and as Lorna rang the on-call paediatrician for an opinion on a sore throat, rather tersely Abby told her that not every child had meningitis, not every child merited bloods and admission, *just in case*. Both women were right and both women were wrong—that was the nature of medicine and Lorna was struggling with it.

Really struggling with it, in fact.

But nothing, not a hellish night at work, or a boss that was out to get her, compared to losing James.

The station was virtually empty at seven-thirty a.m. on a Sunday morning.

She sat on the platform and checked her phone, to see again if he had called her. Though why he would or should, Lorna had no idea. He didn't have to justify himself to her.

And he didn't.

No blinking light on her answering machine when, frozen, she made it home.

Showering and pulling on her mint green pyjamas and the socks of James's she'd kept, she set her alarm and curled up in bed.

Told herself she had to go to sleep because she had to be on the ball for tonight's shift.

Told herself it was good that he was moving on, because now maybe she could.

Told herself that once this wretched operation was over she'd feel better.

Except she couldn't stop crying.

CHAPTER NINETEEN

HER four nights of hell were nearly over and all Lorna wanted was to leave and never return, was seriously considering doing that just as soon as this shift was over.

She'd hardly sat down since nine p.m. and the clock was nearing six, and though she'd gone to have a quick rest in the staffroom she'd found James asleep in there.

He'd been called in three times and had clearly given up on going home. He'd been stretched out over several seats, absolutely zonked out, his mouth slightly open, one hand dangling on the floor, the other on his stomach.

He was wearing theatre blues, and the top had lifted to show just a little glimpse of his stomach. Lorna had sat with her cup of instant soup, trying to concentrate on some early morning TV show, except it sounded like her father preaching, so she'd turned her gaze away and stared at James instead.

At his big feet and his thick thighs, and that lovely floppy fringe, and that chest she loved to bite.

And those lips that had so many times kissed her. Never more had she wanted to wake him with one.

And then she'd stared down at the bit she was avoiding looking at, because one of the advantages or disadvantages of threadbare hospital blues was that you could tell James dressed to the left.

It really wasn't much of a break, so Lorna gave in, rinsed out her cup and headed back out. She settled for gulping a cup of coffee at the nurses' station and, of course, Abby had to dash past at that point on her way to a patient in Resus.

'Do you need a hand?' Lorna called, but Abby just tossed her head.

'Carry on with your break.'

'Call this a break!' Lorna rolled her eyes at Lavinia, who giggled.

'She's a great doctor,' Lavinia said. 'She just rubs people up the wrong way.'

'Even you?' Lorna checked.

'Even me.'

'I know she's a great doctor, I'm living proof after all. I keep reminding myself that she saved my life.'

'She probably regrets it now.'

It was the first time, the very first time, Lorna glimpsed fitting in, the first time she'd shared a joke or chatted easily with the bitchy clique of the emergency team, and all Lorna knew was that she wanted more.

'Right!' Lavinia downed the remains of her mug. 'We'd better get on and clear this place a bit before the day staff get here. It's been a shocking weekend.'

'Has it?'

'Awful!' Lavinia nodded. 'Still, it's nearly over now.'

She touched wood the second she said it, but it was already too late—the alert phone trilled and even as Ambulance control told her there was a paediatric arrest en route, the ambulance was screaming in. Paramedics raced through the department with a loose-limbed little blue bundle and suddenly, for Lorna, the pressure was on.

'Where's Abby?'

'She's in with the aneurism,' May said calmly, her heart sinking as the paramedics laid down their lifeless load. Lorna was bagging the baby as May massaged his chest. 'The paediatricians *are* coming,' she explained, 'but they're stuck on ICU. I've called the second on call and the second anaesthetist.'

'Get James.' Lorna's voice was wobbly, but she said it quite clearly. She wished in fact that James would walk through the door this very second.

'He's just left for home.'

'Call him to come back,' Lorna said.

She'd dealt with death. As a rural GP it was part of her life, and she'd even dealt with babies and children, but they had been so few and far between that as she stared down at the little mottled, white scrap, Lorna wondered just what the hell she was doing here—why anyone would *want* this job, when death was a daily occurrence.

May was delivering massage to the tiny little shell of a life, Lavinia was trying to get IV access and Lorna knew she had to attempt intubation. Often it was done by the time the patient arrived, but in this case the attempt had been unsuccessful and it had been decided to bag the baby and get him to hospital. In the absence of an anaesthetist it was up to her try. She inserted the laryngoscope and suctioned his airway till she could see the epiglottis and vocal cords. She willed herself calm and even though her hands were shaking the tube was passing through and May secured it for her, taking over the bagging as Lorna tried to find a vein on the other fat little arm as Lavinia was having trouble. Her hands were still shaking so violently she must surely miss, but she pushed in the needle and could feel the sweat break out on her brow in sheer relief as she got the little flashback of blood that meant she was in.

'Nice work,' May said, telling Lavinia to tape it securely, then helping Lorna with the tiny drug doses that were required in a paediatric arrest. Lorna was doing well herself, because she had dealt with this before and she had kept herself up to date. She was also so obsessive she had read and re-read the protocol till it was taped to her brain.

'There's blood in the ear canal…' She checked his eyes, saw the damage and for a second closed her own. It was wrong to jump to conclusions, so she deliberately didn't, examining him carefully and drawing on the little diagram. She noticed the swelling on his thigh and the shortened leg that looked as if it was fractured.

She had relatives sobbing in the interview

room, an abused baby who was moribund and she wanted to scoop him up and hold him, only she couldn't. 'Get X-Ray.' They were already there and so, too, thankfully the paediatricians, with James running in behind.

The baby was given every chance, every last chance, but everyone knew he wasn't going to make it. The rush of expertise arrived some fifteen minutes before the little life officially ended, the police were already in with the parents, and Lorna could only stand there as James went in to break the news.

'Do you want to come with me?' It was a stupid question, there wasn't a person on earth who would want to be there, but she knew what he meant, that if this was to be her job then this was the type of conversation she needed to get used to having. The right thing to do would be to say yes, to swallow down the tears that were threatening to choke her, to watch and learn from a more experienced colleague how to deal with the parents and police and myriad conflicting parties before she had to go in and do it by herself—only she couldn't.

'I'd rather not.'

'Lorna.' James voice was firm. 'I'll do the talking. You ought to observe.'

'I'd rather not,' she said again, because she'd *really* rather not.

She was a strange little thing, James thought as he chose to leave it. Like a twig that might snap or break, except that this one bent. According to May, she'd done an outstanding job, which was what mattered the most—it was right that he didn't stretch her to breaking point by having her in with the relatives.

'I'll get him ready for the parents.' May, lovely, lovely May was matter-of-fact but crying quietly as she wrapped him up and held him in her arms, all the tubes staying in place because this was a coroner's case.

'Will they be able to hold him?' Lorna asked, stroking the white cheek and stunned at the speed at which life ended. 'I mean…'

'The courts will decide who's responsible.' May hugged the little boy close. 'Not us. You treat them with dignity and respect even if it kills you inside to do so.'

'Does it kill you inside?' Lorna asked, glad somehow that she'd seen May crying, not that there was much evidence now. May had dabbed at her cheeks with a tissue and was waiting for James to tell her to bring the baby to his family. Lorna was relieved that she wasn't the only one who was utterly devastated by what had just taken place. 'I mean, do you get used to it all?'

'Never.' May said. 'I'd leave if I did.'

Yes, babies died and, yes, it wasn't that rare an occurrence in a busy emergency department, but it was still a subdued team that greeted the day staff. The police and family were still there and the baby was too, and everyone was a little bit gentler on everyone else this morning. In fact, no one complained that she took for ever on her notes. Lorna sat with a big mug of tea and wrote up all that she'd done, even managed a smile at a joke from one of the porters, but her face was so pale, her subtle blusher now looked as if it had been slapped on, two streaks of tawny colour down the side of her face. Her hands were shaking when she handed her notes over to the paediatrician and, despite appearances, James knew she was having trouble holding it together. He couldn't stand the thought of her going home alone to deal with it, instead of letting some of it out here, amongst staff who could give her some support.

When she pulled on her coat, and his on call had officially ended, instead of hanging around to clear the place, he walked through the department with her. He could not let her go home on the underground alone.

And it wasn't just because she was his ex, or maybe it was, but he had to try and talk to her.

'Don't go home yet.'

'I'm tired.' She was clipping out of the department and refusing to slow down.

'You haven't even cried,' James said. 'You cry at everything.'

'If I start, I don't think I'll stop.'

'You will,' James promised. 'You need to go over it, Lorna.'

'Why?' she snapped. 'Is it going to bring him back?' She was almost running now, but he caught her arm and made her stop, stood in the corridor outside Emergency, which at nine a.m. was crowded with people, and it was neither the time nor the place. Lorna told him as much as he bundled her into a small annexe beside the admissions desk. 'I'm not surprised that you're having trouble holding onto doctors. My shift ended more than an hour ago.'

'Talk to me, Lorna.'

'No, because I'm tired and I just want to go to bed. I don't need some touchy-feely session to tell me that what I'm feeling is normal or to give me permission to be angry.'

'No, you don't,' James said, letting her go, because he *was* crossing the line but, hell, it was hard to be just a colleague around her and it was killing him to let her go home to cry alone. 'But you do need to—'

'I need to go home,' she said. 'Away from this place. I'm tired of being made to feel useless, I'm tired of being told I'm too slow and I'm too cautious.'

'You're doing well.'

'Oh, please,' Lorna scoffed. 'I'll be told off now for calling you in without Abby's permission, no doubt!'

'Abby spoke to me before. She said you've really picked up. She told me about the perforated ulcer and how you noticed it when she didn't.'

'She told you?'

'And you know you did a good job with that baby.'

'Not good enough, though.'

'Lorna, no one could have saved him. Do you realise what a good job you did in there? You intubated him, you got IV access. You with your shaking hands who'd miss one of my veins managed to get it in to a collapsed baby.'

'How?' She asked the bit that she truly didn't understand, the bit that terrified her most, the bit she was certain she could never do. 'How can you talk to them, be nice to them, when you know…?'

'We don't know, Lorna.'

'Please.' She knew not to jump to conclusions, had been very careful not to when she'd been assessing the patient, but now, having read the little boy's medical history, both of them deep down knew the truth. 'How can you sit in there with them and be polite, knowing what's gone on?'

'Because for me it's easier,' James said. 'Because, like you with your crying, if I started saying all the things I actually wanted to say, then I'm sure I'd never stop.'

He'd always loved kids, had teased her at the start of her marriage that he wanted five at least, and he'd have been such a brilliant father. It was hard to believe that ten years on he wasn't one yet and it was over between them, except for one thing—except for the one thing they'd never, ever been able to discuss.

And maybe it was because they were finally over, or maybe it was because she was exhausted and drained and weeping inside for that waste of a little boy's life, that for the first time she said it.

'We'd have been such good parents.' Even though he wasn't pushing her to talk now, even though she could walk away, she chose not to. The floodgates crashed open and pointless as it was because that was just the way life was, finally she said it. 'It's not *fair,* James.'

CHAPTER TWENTY

PAULINE was vacuuming when James opened the door, but her bright smile faded the second she saw Lorna, pale and shivering, beside him.

'James, I've got the most terrible migraine,' she said. 'I'm going to have to go home.'

'That's fine.'

'I've put the dishwasher on.'

'That's fine, Pauline,' James said, relieved that she was going. This ten years overdue conversation didn't need an audience.

'It's not fair.' Lorna sat on the sofa and said it again. 'Why couldn't our baby have lived?'

'Because it couldn't,' James said sitting beside her, holding her frozen hands. 'Because it didn't…'

'I know it was ages ago, I know I should be over it, I am over it.' She screwed her face up as she tried to explain. 'I just... Seeing that little baby...'

'We all feel it,' James said. 'And it isn't fair, because we'd have loved ours so much.' And the tears started then, but they were different tears from her usual ones. Her usual tears were silent and frequent, a little river that flowed easily, while this was like a dam bursting, an outpouring that had even James wondering if she *would* ever stop. He held her body as she cried, not just for the little baby this morning but for her baby, for their baby that they'd never even got to hold.

'I don't even know what it was. I didn't ask, I didn't.' She was bent over double on the chair and he was holding her shoulders, had been for the last hour now.

'A girl.' James said, because ten years on they could finally talk about it. 'It was a little girl that we lost.'

And it was nice to cry together, horrible and sad but nice. It was good to hold each other and weep for their little girl who should be dashing off to school right now, who would have been so very loved if only she had lived. It was good, James thought, to be able to *say* it, to let Lorna know that he really had cared, that it had made him bleed too, but on the inside.

And even if they thought she'd never stop crying, of course Lorna did, beating the dishwasher to the end of its cycle, in fact. She let James hold her and listened to the noise of his empty house the gurgle of the dishwasher draining. Lorna was just *being* for a moment instead of thinking, until James spoke.

'I love you Lorna.' She froze in his arms, wished he wouldn't say it. 'I always have and I always will.'

'You said you didn't.'

'No.' He would say it this time, would tell her what he'd tried to all those years ago. 'I said in a row that I felt trapped, and I did feel trapped, because I was twenty-five and we'd barely started going out and your parents insisted we marry. I did feel trapped, because you lost the baby and then you hated me.'

'No.'

'Yes,' James countered. 'You just lay on that couch and looked at me as if you hated me.'

'No.'

'Yes!' James insisted, because she had. 'And then we'd row and then you dragged it out of me that I didn't love you on our wedding day. Hell, Lorna, I didn't know you on our wedding day and,' he admitted, because he was going to be honest now, 'I didn't know *how* to love you once we lost the baby. I'll tell you when I realised I loved you. The minute you walked out that door, the second I lost you, I realised how much I loved you, only you didn't want to hear it. You went back to your parents and let them brainwash you some more.'

'No.'

'Yes,' James said, but this time she was adamant.

'No,' Lorna said again. 'I did go back to Scotland and I stood up to him. I told him I wasn't a whore because I'd had sex out of wedlock, I told him what a good man you were and that divorce wasn't a sin—that it just didn't work out.'

'You said that?'

'Yes.' And he held her tight because he knew how hard that would have been. 'And I believed it too. We didn't speak for years after that. But, James...' Oh, this was hard, this was so hard. 'I loved you so much, I loved you from the first day of medical school and I set my cap at you that night.'

'Lorna.'

'No, listen. That night I dressed for you, I put on make-up and perfume and I set out to get you to notice me.'

'Lorna!' He halted her then, stopped the rotten legacy her father had given her in its tracks. 'That's called flirting. That's what people do when they like each other. You're not some witch who cast a spell on me that night. I was crazy about you too.'

'I didn't expect it to be so-o-o…' She screwed her face up as she tried to explain. 'I never thought it would be so much, that we'd want each other so much!'

And even if it was jumbled, he *did* understand. Because they hadn't just flirted, they'd connected that night, connected at a level James had spent the last decade trying to recapture. They'd entered a world where they spoke in a new language, cracked the code, discovered new colours. His twenty-two-year-old virgin had unlocked the door and unleashed a tiger, and she blamed herself for it.

'I set out to hook you that night and I did, and I got the prize—you married me for the baby, and suddenly there wasn't one. You did marry me for the baby, James.'

'Yes,' he admitted. 'But I also believe we'd

have got there in the end anyway.' He felt the shift in her then, could almost see the mist clearing as she stared back at their past and took away all the hurt and pain that had led them to this. 'I've never been happier than you made me, Lorna.' And now ten years on surely he could say it. 'And I'm sorry we couldn't talk about the baby, but we are now, and there *will* be others.' It was the worst thing to say to a woman who had lost a child, but this was ten years on, he knew that. Surely it was okay now, but seeing her stricken face he could have kicked himself for saying it. 'You're thirty-three, Lorna.'

'There'll be no others.' And out it came. If she'd been upset before it was nothing to this. 'He said my sins would catch up with me and I didn't believe him. I know that I did nothing wrong, I'm a doctor for God's sake, but that year, that horrible year, when I went back to the doctors each time, I felt as if my sins *were* catching up with me. Adhesions from my appendix, endometriosis… I'm a mess inside, James. There won't be any more babies.'

'You don't know that.'

'I do!' Lorna sobbed. 'Because I can't live with the pain, and in four weeks' time I'm having a hysterectomy.'

And it was out and she'd said it and he was still holding her.

He never wanted to stop holding her—here in his living room, his head felt as if it was imploding. There was a tumble of regret, of anger, about wasted, wasted years and wasted, wasted futures, about the damage that had been done, not just this morning to the baby they had fought to save but to the woman he was holding in his arms now. He knew she was spent now, knew he needed to think before he rushed in and said the wrong thing, so instead he stood her up and said the only thing he knew that she wanted to hear.

'Bed.'

He gave her his *nice man* kiss, a little kiss on the forehead that told her he knew she was tired, drained, utterly exhausted. He took her upstairs, unbuttoned her coat, took off her clothes and his own. He pulled the duvet over and pulled her into his arms and held her, didn't say a word as it all sank in. He held her the same way he had the night her father had screamed at them and told her she was a slut and a whore, the same way he had the night she'd come home after losing their baby.

Their little girl.

Lorna was thinking about her too.

'Is she the L on your keying?'

'She's the one,' James said.

'Lily.'

There were no tears left, just relief at being able to finally mourn *her* and the shrivelling sorrow for the baby that had died today too. Then there was James, his hand low on her stomach as if somehow he loved it—adhesions and endometriosis and missing Fallopian tube and all.

As if somehow still he loved her.

CHAPTER TWENTY-ONE

LORNA had no idea what time it was when she awoke. For a while she lay there, his body spooned into hers, not trying to orientate herself, suspended in whatever time it was and remembering.

The hellish night shift.

Telling him her truth.

And waking in his arms.

Oh, James was too much of a gentleman to baulk and run. Lying there, she almost braced herself for a talking-to, that he cared for her, that he always would, but it was ten years ago now... But his warm palm was pressing harder into her breast, and his mouth was on the back of her shoulder and for a moment she wondered if she had actually told him because it seemed as if nothing had changed, as if, even with the truth, he still wanted her.

And then she stopped thinking, turned over in the darkness and faced him, kissed him on his lips and meshed her skin with his. It didn't matter if it was morning, afternoon or evening, because time took on a new meaning when she was in his arms.

He sort of tumbled her onto her back and he was still kissing her. He could be almost matter-of-fact at times in his love-making, but in a delicious way that drove her wild. As if her body were dotted with Braille he read it, taking his weight on his elbows, parting her warm legs with his knees. And who the hell needed foreplay? Because as he slipped inside her she was ready anyway, ready for James to take his time. He didn't say a word and neither did Lorna. They revelled in each other's bodies, and whoever said the missionary position was boring hadn't been a devotee of James. There was no rush, just a lovely languorous journey, where she crept out of her mind as he crept inside her body, accepting the sensations he afforded—the slide of his skin over hers, the taste of his chest, her hands slid down his torso in their own lazy time then felt his taut buttocks and dug him deeper inside her. She loved his ragged breathing in her ear, loved the weight pressing down on her, but he was being too gentle, mindful of her chest when he didn't have to be any more. Or maybe he did, because it hurt just a little but he solved that in an instant, wrapping his arms under her now, so she got the contact but not the weight, and it was so nice she wanted to stay there for ever.

She wished she could stop moaning, because she didn't want to signal the end, wished she could tell her hands to stop digging into him and her legs to stop tightening around him because she never wanted him to stop. He didn't. Even as she was coming, still he drove her further, and it was delicious, like gorging yourself on chocolate ice cream and going back to find the freezer still full. Still he was there, still he was driving into her, and if James's control was to be admired, she had absolutely none, and for a minister's daughter her language was shocking. She'd have to have a quiet word to herself later. James did not seem to mind, he *obviously* didn't, in fact, because as her orgasm hit again he forgot to be gentle now, held her so tight as he thrust inside her, muffled her words with his chest and took her—because he could.

'You want babies,' Lorna said into the darkness. Having made love in his very dark bedroom, they were lying there all wrapped up and content, and when it came around, it was nice to find out they were big enough and able enough to talk about it now.

'I want lots of things,' James said, 'but I want you more.'

'We could adopt.'

'We can do lots of things.' James agreed.

'I'm worried.' She took a big breath and blew it out and tested flying with her new honest wings. 'I'm worried that I'll get depressed again after the operation, that I'll put you through it all over again.'

'You won't,' James said, 'because I'll drag those dark thoughts out of you and you'll talk to me this time, and you'll see someone if you have to. Lorna, if you knew the hell of these past years. I've been trying to find you, find a woman that made me laugh, that fitted…'

'James!'

'We fit,' James said. 'We just did, till you went all dark on me.'

'We did,' Lorna agreed, then addressed a nagging guilt. 'What about Ellie? That was more…'

'It was,' he admitted.

'What will you tell her?' Her body swept with dread, because Ellie hadn't entered her head till now, and that he'd hurt her once over Lorna was bad enough, but that he'd hurt her twice was unthinkable.

'Tell her?' He could feel her cringe and then he remembered that little look in Resus, where she'd got it all wrong, and he'd chosen, though it had been hard to do so, to not put her right— but he could now.

Could, because finally they were being honest.

'She asked if we could go out for dinner— there was something she had to say. So I went, I owed her that.'

'You did,' Lorna admitted. 'So what did she say?'

'A lot!' James rolled his eyes in the darkness. 'I was never into her, I never took her to work things, we'd been going out a year and I'd never even hinted that she move in, I was too wrapped up in work. She gave me a right earful actually. Then she said she deserved better, which I agreed with, and then Abby rang and asked me to come in, which she said proved her point exactly, so she took the phone, gave Abby an earful and then stomped out of the restaurant and I paid for dinner.'

'Oh.'

'I'm rubbish in bed too, by the way.' James added glumly. 'It wasn't a great night, but it had to be done.'

'She'll be okay.'

'She will be,' James said, 'because she was right. She did deserve better. Now…' He rolled on his side and faced her. 'About you. You're going to see Henry Lowther. He's the best gynaecologist—'

'I've had second, third, fourth opinions,' Lorna said.

'Good, but Henry's the best and he'll do a wonderful job and hopefully sort out those adhesions too. Is that why you were on so many painkillers?' He kissed her forehead when she nodded. 'Well, you won't be soon. You shouldn't have to live in pain.'

And he was so nice and so accepting of it that it turned out there were some tears left after all.

'It's been a bit better,' she admitted. 'A lot better, actually—like going to the dentist and suddenly your toothache's gone.'

'Go and see Henry.'

'He's at the same hospital, though.' Lorna cringed but James just laughed.

'I'm sure he's seen it all before!'

He had.

He waded through her medical history, which was as thick as a telephone book from the car accident alone, looked at all her scans and reports and medications and then he examined her.

'Hmm.' He was one of those eccentric old-school doctors who wore a bow-tie on a Tuesday. 'I will want to have a look before I proceed to a hysterectomy.' This made her groan because so many doctors had had so many looks. 'You still look a bit anaemic. I'll run some bloods but I'd like you to up your iron, and my secretary will arrange an ultra-sound, then I'd like to do a quick laparoscopy and have a look before we decide how to proceed.'

And she was about to say no, to just go with the doctor she was with, because she'd been through it so very many times, but he was rather thorough and reassuring, and it was her only womb and, yes, as she rolled up her sleeve and the needle slid in, Lorna knew that even if it just made James realise she'd done everything, it was worth just a bit more discomfort.

CHAPTER TWENTY-TWO

'THERE, there, pet.' May chatted away to Rita who was back for a pap smear.

Emergency wasn't really the place for such a routine procedure, Lorna knew that and Abby had also wasted no time pointing it out, but she left Lorna to get on with it and for Lorna it was good to see that Rita was taking care of herself. She'd specifically asked for the Scottish doctor, she hadn't even added 'posh,' and as was often the case, it wasn't just the pap smear she was there for. As Lorna asked the right questions a couple of other problems Lorna was expecting cropped up.

'I'm going to get the gynaecologist to come down and talk to you,' Lorna said when Rita was sitting up with her blanket back on. 'There are lots of different treatments…'

'Is it a male or female doctor?'

'Lowther's team,' May said, because she knew things like that without checking.

'He's got a female registrar.' Lorna smiled. 'I'll page her and ask if she can come down.'

'Can't I just make an appointment?' Rita asked, but Lorna didn't want her flying out of the door never to return.

'Let me just have a word with her.'

May was heading off to the canteen for lunch as Lorna wrote her notes. 'Can I get you anything?'

'Roast beef, spinach and horseradish roll with a bottle of orange juice, please.'

'Good girl!' May clucked, taking the money and picking up the ringing phone, then putting on her posh voice for a moment. 'It's Lowther…'

'I haven't paged him yet.' Lorna frowned. 'Anyway I want his reg.' Her voice faded as she took the phone, tears pricking her eyes as she listened to his calm, matter-of-fact voice, and her hand was shaking too much to put back the phone so May did it for her.

'He wants to see me.'

'That's okay.'

'No. I've had some tests.'

'And no doubt your iron's in your boots. I could have told you that from just looking at you.'

'A consultant wouldn't call for that.' She had never been more scared, terrified at what he might have found.

'You're a doctor,' May calmly pointed out. 'He probably thinks he's doing you a courtesy, not scaring the living daylights out of you. Now…' Ever practical, ever calm, she sorted things out. 'Ring the reg and get poor Rita seen, then I'll walk you up to Lowther's rooms.'

Lorna was glad James wasn't on duty. She wanted to deal with whatever it was herself first, instead of worrying him. But the cloud she'd been walking on these last few days seemed to have dissipated. Her legs were like lead as she walked along the long corridors, with May chatting away beside her, trying to keep her mind off things, except nothing would.

'Will we be keeping you?' May asked, as they sat outside his room and Lorna waited to go in. 'You've really picked up in these last weeks.'

'I'm not sure…' Distracted, only half listening, Lorna's brain struggled to work out an answer. James had suggested she stay on, but both wanted to talk properly about the dynamics of working and living together.

Living together. Her head tightened as she recalled the bliss she'd awoken to that morning and she didn't want to shatter it, didn't want Henry Lowther piercing their fragile new dream of having found each other.

She was holding her keys, holding the silver L he had bought for her. She had never felt more alone in her life; she had to talk to May. 'I'm having a hysterectomy soon.' Her terrified eyes turned to May's who just gave her a soft, sad smile that helped. 'I've got so many medical problems, I'm so scared, May. Maybe I *should* call James…' She clamped her mouth closed because they had decided to keep it quiet, but she knew he'd forgive her, knew she hadn't just blurted it out on her morning coffee break. 'We're sort of back together.'

'Tell me something I don't know!' May smiled. 'Now, just let's hear what Lowther has to say before you go worrying about something you don't know about,' May said. 'He's a wonderful doctor. I've been in for a service and repair with him a few times myself, there's no man more thorough. Do you want me to come in with you?'

Intensely private, Lorna shook her head, but when May squeezed her hand as the secretary called for her to go in, Lorna changed her mind. 'Please.'

It was the longest walk of her life.

CHAPTER TWENTY-THREE

'I LIKE to be thorough,' Henry said as they both took a seat. May was reverential in front of the great man himself. 'After I examined you I had my suspicions so I took the precaution of running a BHCG…a pregnancy test,' he explained, as Lorna just frowned at him. 'And the levels were high.'

'I can't be.'

'I understand that this is a shock,' Henry Lowther said, 'and I also understand that with your history it might be wise not to get too excited, so I want you to have a quick ultrasound before we continue.' He pointed to his treatment bed and Lorna just sat there at first, and then was grateful May *had* come in with her, because she couldn't have made it to the bed by herself. May led her over and pulled the screen, clucked and fussed and helped her with the zipper on her skirt, then folded her clothes. She chatted away about wool-blend skirts and the very nice lining until the doctor came round, and then she held Lorna's hand.

'Good girl!' she rabbited on. 'Just a bit of cold jelly on your stomach.'

Lorna didn't want to look and she didn't dare to hope, could hear the rapid whoosh, whoosh of a little heartbeat that meant he wasn't playing some sick joke, which of course she knew he wasn't. But a heartbeat didn't mean a bean if it wasn't in the right place. Now he was running the probe to her left, she knew it was over her remaining Fallopian tube. Surely God couldn't be cruel enough to do it to her again.

'Just checking there's not another one anywhere…'

'Thorough!' May mouthed to Lorna as her eyes darted in alarm.

Thorough's good, Lorna decided, thorough she liked, especially when he said the words she wanted to hear.

'Just one…nice and high up in the uterus.'

'I'm pregnant.'

'Congratulations.' It was the best word in the world and he said it again, and May said it too.

'I'm on the Pill,' Lorna said, because she couldn't be pregnant, because even with the photo he was peeling off, she wouldn't let herself believe it.

'Well, *Doctor.*' Henry smiled. 'The Pill can be affected by antibiotics and you had a course…'

'Sweet Lord above us.' May smiled. 'So you did—I dispensed them myself!'

'You're still fertile, Lorna,' Henry said. 'Yes, with only one Fallopian tube it halves the odds, and the adhesions and endometrioses, yes, it could be difficult, but clearly that ovary is working just fine and your left tube must be clear. You said you'd been feeling better recently?'

It was starting to sink in.

'She's eating like a horse.' May grinned as Henry went back to his desk. 'I knew that you were pregnant, I've known for days.'

'You did not,' Lorna scoffed.

'I did so!' May insisted. 'I didn't know all about your troubles. You've been glowing these past days.'

'That was the sex!' Lorna whispered, and the two women almost fell to the floor laughing. There was a wonderful euphoria, a sort of lightness, a looseness that Lorna had longed for, and now she wanted to share it with James.

'Go home,' May said, when Lorna had thanked and thanked and thanked Henry Lowther and booked her first antenatal appointment.

Antenatal appointment!

She wanted to kiss the bored receptionist's face as she handed her her card.

'I'm on till five.'

'Go home!' May said again, and Lorna nodded, butterflies dancing in her stomach, but duty still called. 'I'll just have a quick word with Rita and then I'll go…'

To tell James.

CHAPTER TWENTY-FOUR

PUT champagne in fridge!!!!!!

Pauline frowned at May's text.

Am working! she replied.

I know just do it x

So she did as she was told and hovered in the living room, watching her self-help show as James worked in the garden. Spring would soon be springing and he was sorting out the tiny courtyard, which meant she could just sit down and watch the end of her favourite show.

She didn't mean to fall asleep. She jumped up when Lorna walked in and apologised profusely.

'It's fine.' For once Lorna's face was smiling. 'Why don't you just finish up for today, Pauline.' As Pauline opened her mouth to argue,

Lorna was still smiling. 'We'll cover the hours. I know you do loads extra. Where *is* James?'

'Out in the garden,' Pauline said, pulling on her coat and opening the front door as Lorna said goodbye and headed to the back.

And Pauline would have gone, but she'd left her glasses by the living-room table so she walked back and stood, watched as Lorna walked over to James. Pauline saw him smile and frown at the same time at Lorna's unexpected early arrival and stop what he was doing. Pauline was tempted so tempted to stand and watch for a little while longer—but it wasn't her business, so instead she left them to it and quietly headed out onto the street.

Then she pulled out her phone and rang May.

'Hey?' Lorna could hear the question in his voice as she walked over. 'What are you doing home?'

'I couldn't stand the place a moment longer.' She would have played along for a little while more, except she couldn't keep the smile from her face. 'Henry Lowther asked me to come and see him.'

'And you're smiling?' He was too now. 'Does he think you might not need the operation after all?'

'I probably will need it,' Lorna said, 'just not for a while. For a few months, in fact.'

'And you're okay with that?' James checked. 'You said the pain…'

'I haven't been in much pain for a few weeks now,' Lorna said. 'Even when I came off the medication after the accident.' She thought he'd get it, thought he'd work it out before she even told him, but it had seemed such an impossible dream, something just so out of reach, she understood why his mind hadn't gone there.

It meant she had to tell him and the words just rushed out of her, spilled out of her mouth because she had to share the news and share it this very instant, because he deserved every second of this wonderful joy that was as much his news too.

'I'm pregnant.' She never thought she'd say it again and especially to him. 'I've had an ultrasound and the position is good.'

And James had so completely accepted they were words he'd never hear, especially from Lorna, that it took a while for them to sink in. James had quietly dealt with the grief of never having children because, though he'd never, ever tell Lorna, there *had* been a sense of loss when he'd found out about her operation. And though the grief was merited, it was also completely worth it if it meant he had Lorna. Still, there had been a loss to deal with privately just the same.

'It's going to be fine,' Lorna said, not smiling now, not even crying as he took her in his arms. 'I'm not even scared, James. I just know it's going to be alright.'

'It will be.' He kissed her then, a kiss she didn't have a name for, a kiss she had never tasted till now. It tasted of endings and beginnings, of past and of future, and it tasted of love and passion, but there was another ingredient too and as they walked into the house Lorna worked out what it was.

Hope.

She sat at the kitchen table and stared at her antenatal card, at her due date and LMP and her next scheduled appointment. The thin wintry sun was streaming through the window and she let *hope* sink in as James headed to the fridge to make her lunch because even if it was the most wonderful moment, she'd just remembered she was starving and dying for a cup of tea.

Oh, there was chance and there were risks and a lot of negatives if you chose to look for them, but then there was faith and that was a much kinder path to follow. There was faith that all was right with the world, that someone, somewhere *was* looking out for you.

'I can't believe this!' James's voice roused her from her introspection.

'Neither can I.'

'Not that.' James grinned. 'This!' He pulled

a bottle of champagne out of the fridge. 'How on earth did that get there?'

'It just did,' Lorna said, talking about the champagne and the baby and cars that collided and lives that kept living even against the most terrible odds. 'It just is!'

EPILOGUE

JAMES didn't need to be married to her to love her.

A nice guy perhaps, but he was still human and there was a small part of him that would take certain pleasure in living in sin with Minister McClelland's daughter. But he loved Lorna more than he hated her father, so he suggested a registry office wedding—a nice quick service to make things official, with just a couple of witnesses from the street, and then they would tell everybody afterwards.

Only Lorna wanted a church.

And the more he thought about it, the more James wanted one too, because not only would the two different photos of their weddings look great on the mantelpiece and be a talking point for ever, he had a lot to be thankful for.

An awful lot.

And even though they'd intended to make it the smallest of ceremonies, there were a lot of people that wanted to share their joy, so the numbers swelled along with Lorna's stomach, but she had this strange logic that she didn't want people to think they were marrying just because she was having a baby, so the service was duly delayed, to her father's horror.

But Lorna didn't care.

This was her life, her marriage and, as she told her father on the phone one night as James pretended to be watching television, it was her God too.

And it was casual but it was formal, a lovely mix of faces that greeted them as they entered the church.

Together.

James would walk her down the aisle this time and there was no need for her to be given away, she'd been given to him years ago and, despite the time gap, in reality she'd never left.

No, three of them walked down the aisle.

James in a suit, but not a new one, and Lorna in a soft lilac dress that was new, but she'd bought it on an auction web site and had saved a fortune. It was money they needed to save, because they were fast outgrowing his little town house and had their sights set on this vast sprawling home in St John's Wood, or that was the intention. They were trying to squeeze in just one more baby before Lorna had her operation, but whatever the outcome they knew they were already blessed.

So they faced the future as a family, James holding little James, or JJ as he was starting to be known now. The baby's blue eyes were already turning green and his blond hair, or so Lorna insisted, looked decidedly ginger. Lorna held a single lily, which meant nothing to everyone else but everything to them.

And it was the best wedding in the world. Even Minister McClelland managed to crack a smile as he welcomed James back into the fold, while holding his grandson, because at three months old with a smile that would light up London, JJ could soften even the hardest heart. Betty let her hair down for once and drank champagne and danced and then danced some more!

'Won't it be confusing?' Pauline asked as Lorna and James sat at their table and caught up with all of their guests. 'Two Dr Morrells working in the same department?'

'James is Mister,' Abby said, topping up her glass.

'Anyway, female doctors usually keep their maiden names,' May explained. 'So there will be no confusion.'

'Not this one.' Lorna drained her glass. 'I'm going to be Morrell on everything; I'm changing my name this time. Sorry, guys…' she smiled at the momentarily crestfallen faces because it *would* be confusing, but guess what? She didn't care! She was James's wife and wanted everyone to know it.

'Come on, May.' Pauline stood up as a rather energetic number came on. 'I love this song.'

'They're getting on really well.' James grinned as the two of them caused quite a storm on the dance floor. 'It's good we sat them together—you'd think they'd known each other all their lives.' He pulled his new wife onto the dance floor.

'Er, James…' The music was slowing, and it felt as if they were the only two dancing. It was bliss to be in his arms at the end of their perfect day. And it was time to tell him what she'd worked out some time ago, that they were being looked out for and looked after, but that fate needed a helping hand sometimes. Bottles of champagne didn't appear in the fridge for no reason.

'What?'

She was about to tell him but she halted herself. Why spoil it? Lorna thought, staring up into his logical green eyes that, if she told him, would then discount the miracle that actually *had* occurred.

So she told him she loved him instead.

'I know that.' He buried his head in her hair and smelt the lavender of her shampoo and felt the bony angles of her body that fitted perfectly with his, and couldn't believe he'd got so lucky. 'But tell me again.'

So she did.

And she would.

For ever and ever.

MEDICAL™

Large Print

Titles for the next six months…

March

SECRET SHEIKH, SECRET BABY	Carol Marinelli
PREGNANT MIDWIFE: FATHER NEEDED	Fiona McArthur
HIS BABY BOMBSHELL	Jessica Matthews
FOUND: A MOTHER FOR HIS SON	Dianne Drake
THE PLAYBOY DOCTOR'S SURPRISE PROPOSAL	Anne Fraser
HIRED: GP AND WIFE	Judy Campbell

April

ITALIAN DOCTOR, DREAM PROPOSAL	Margaret McDonagh
WANTED: A FATHER FOR HER TWINS	Emily Forbes
BRIDE ON THE CHILDREN'S WARD	Lucy Clark
MARRIAGE REUNITED: BABY ON THE WAY	Sharon Archer
THE REBEL OF PENHALLY BAY	Caroline Anderson
MARRYING THE PLAYBOY DOCTOR	Laura Iding

May

COUNTRY MIDWIFE, CHRISTMAS BRIDE	Abigail Gordon
GREEK DOCTOR: ONE MAGICAL CHRISTMAS	Meredith Webber
HER BABY OUT OF THE BLUE	Alison Roberts
A DOCTOR, A NURSE: A CHRISTMAS BABY	Amy Andrews
SPANISH DOCTOR, PREGNANT MIDWIFE	Anne Fraser
EXPECTING A CHRISTMAS MIRACLE	Laura Iding

MILLS & BOON®

MEDICAL™

Large Print

June

SNOWBOUND: MIRACLE MARRIAGE	Sarah Morgan
CHRISTMAS EVE: DOORSTEP DELIVERY	Sarah Morgan
HOT-SHOT DOC, CHRISTMAS BRIDE	Joanna Neil
CHRISTMAS AT RIVERCUT MANOR	Gill Sanderson
FALLING FOR THE PLAYBOY MILLIONAIRE	Kate Hardy
THE SURGEON'S NEW-YEAR WEDDING WISH	Laura Iding

July

POSH DOC, SOCIETY WEDDING	Joanna Neil
THE DOCTOR'S REBEL KNIGHT	Melanie Milburne
A MOTHER FOR THE ITALIAN'S TWINS	Margaret McDonagh
THEIR BABY SURPRISE	Jennifer Taylor
NEW BOSS, NEW-YEAR BRIDE	Lucy Clark
GREEK DOCTOR CLAIMS HIS BRIDE	Margaret Barker

August

EMERGENCY: PARENTS NEEDED	Jessica Matthews
A BABY TO CARE FOR	Lucy Clark
PLAYBOY SURGEON, TOP-NOTCH DAD	Janice Lynn
ONE SUMMER IN SANTA FE	Molly Evans
ONE TINY MIRACLE…	Carol Marinelli
MIDWIFE IN A MILLION	Fiona McArthur

MILLS & BOON®

millsandboon.co.uk Community

Join Us!

The Community is the perfect place to meet and chat to kindred spirits who love books and reading as much as you do, but it's also the place to:

- ■ **Get the inside scoop from authors about their latest books**
- ■ **Learn how to write a romance book with advice from our editors**
- ■ **Help us to continue publishing the best in women's fiction**
- ■ **Share your thoughts on the books we publish**
- ■ **Befriend other users**

Forums: Interact with each other as well as authors, editors and a whole host of other users worldwide.

Blogs: Every registered community member has their own blog to tell the world what they're up to and what's on their mind.

Book Challenge: We're aiming to read 5,000 books and have joined forces with The Reading Agency in our inaugural Book Challenge.

Profile Page: Showcase yourself and keep a record of your recent community activity.

Social Networking: We've added buttons at the end of every post to share via digg, Facebook, Google, Yahoo, technorati and de.licio.us.

www.millsandboon.co.uk